HOW TO READ BASS CLEF ON THE PIANO

A Musician's Guide and Workbook for the Left Hand

By Caroline McCaskey and Charylu Ro

All arrangements by Caroline McCaskey and Charylu Roberts
Book Design by Charylu Roberts, O.Ruby Productions
Graphic/Production Assistance: Nicola Marchi
Editing: Ronny S. Schiff, Wendy DeWitt and Matt Wolf

ISBN 978-1-5400-9164-2

Visit Hal Leonard Online at
www.halleonard.com

Contact us:
Hal Leonard
7777 West Bluemound Road
Milwaukee, WI 53213
Email: info@halleonard.com

In Europe, contact:
Hal Leonard Europe Limited
42 Wigmore Street
Marylebone, London, W1U 2RN
Email: info@halleonardeurope.com

In Australia, contact:
Hal Leonard Australia Pty. Ltd.
4 Lentara Court
Cheltenham, Victoria, 3192 Australia
Email: info@halleonard.com.au

PREFACE

This book is for piano students who already have a beginning knowledge of reading and playing music (basic rhythms, time signatures and an understanding of the musical alphabet) but have struggled with the left hand and the bass clef. It is perfect for students of treble clef instruments who want to be able to play the piano and need extra support in the process of learning to read bass clef for the first time. It is also an excellent resource for singers who would like to know the left hand better in order to accompany themselves.

By introducing only a few notes at a time and thoroughly reinforcing them with a variety of exercises and songs, this comprehensive workbook will enable reading the bass clef comfortably from a very low G (three ledger lines below the bass clef staff) to E above middle C (two ledger lines above the bass clef staff).

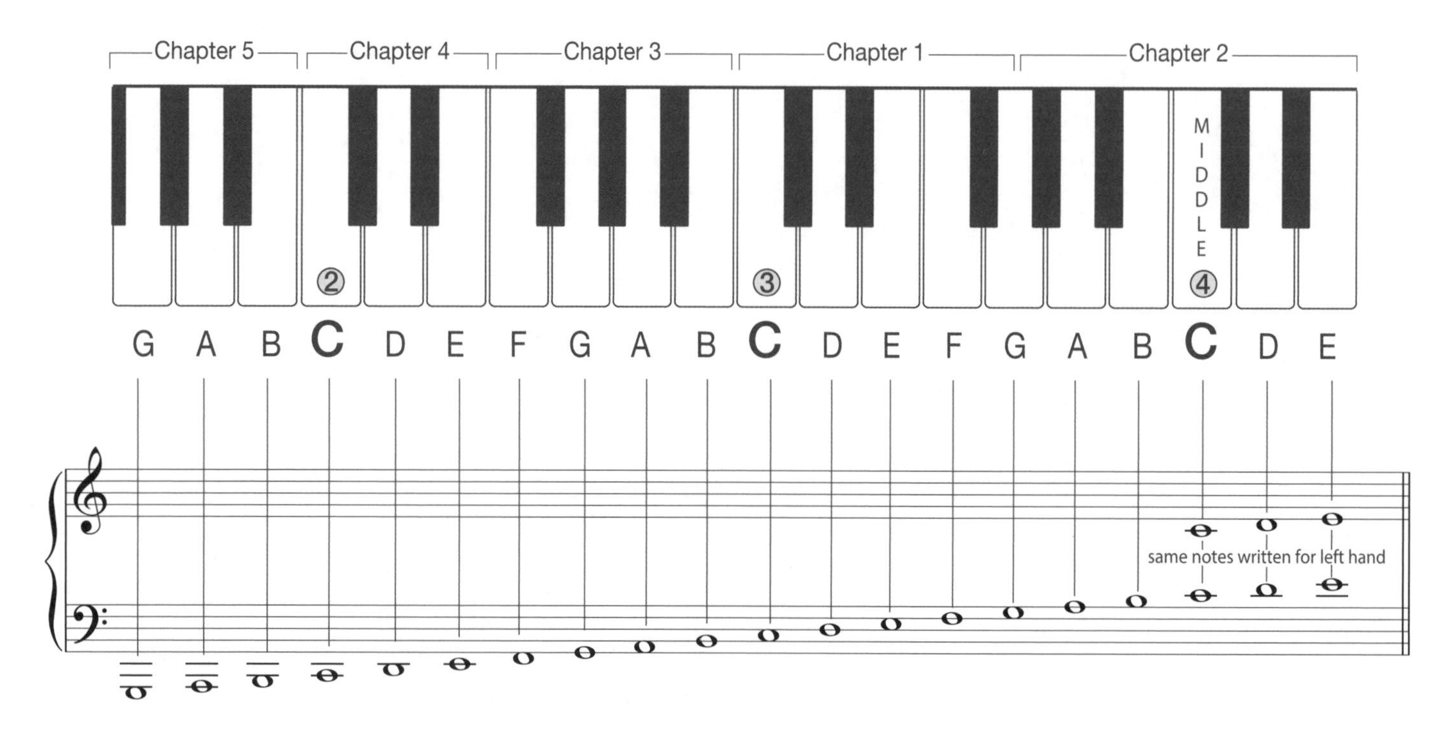

You may feel overwhelmed, but by the end of this book, you will comfortably recognize each of these notes. If this is your goal, you've come to the right place!

To designate all the different octaves of the note C on the piano, an international standard is used called *International Pitch Notation* (IPN) or *Scientific Pitch Notation* (SPN). It labels middle C as C4 (the fourth C on the piano), the C below middle C as C3, etc. However, many piano students today learn on shortened keyboards (60 or 76 keys instead of a full 88 keys). To prevent confusion, this book refers to the C below middle C (C3) as "Bass C" and refers to two octaves below middle C (C2) as "Low C."

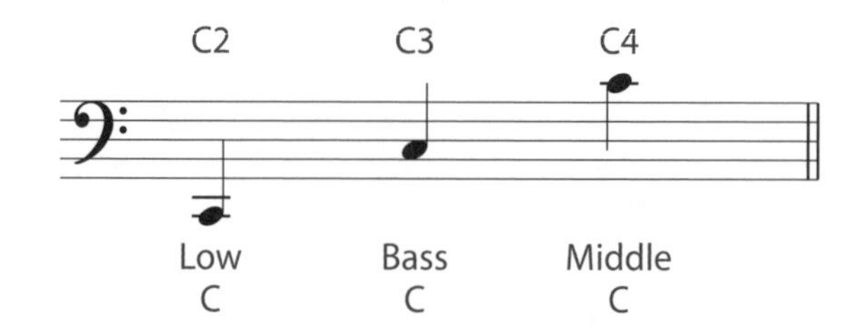

Because accompaniment is such an important function of the left hand, each chapter includes common accompaniment patterns and basic chord progressions taken from real music. As you progress, the accompaniment patterns become more complex, progressing to bass lines and examples found in jazz, boogie-woogie, rock, pop and contemporary styles.

CONTENTS

HISTORY OF THE BASS CLEF

The modern system of the five-line staff came into widespread use in the 16th century, and as a result, clefs began to be used to indicate the notes on the staff. Although there are many clefs in use today by performers of early music, the four clefs you may encounter (from highest to lowest) are treble, alto, tenor, and bass clef.

Here is middle C in each of the four clefs:

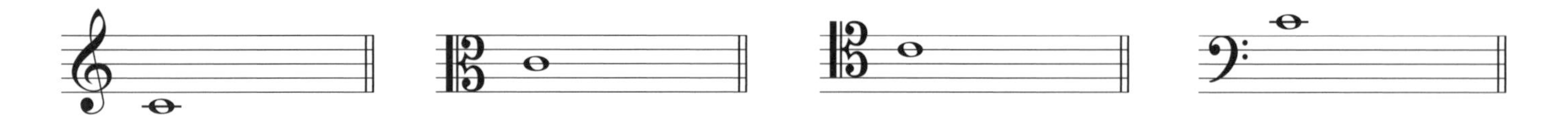

As you can see, middle C is depicted higher in the bass clef than in the others. That means there is more room for lower notes within the lines of the bass clef staff.

How We Read the Bass Clef

Our modern day clefs were originally letters of the alphabet. The bass clef symbol itself came from a stylized letter F (shown above). Although it looks different today, the bass clef symbol still shows us where F is on the staff. Reading from the bottom: the fourth line of the bass clef staff is F, and it passes through the two dots in the bass clef. F marks the spot!

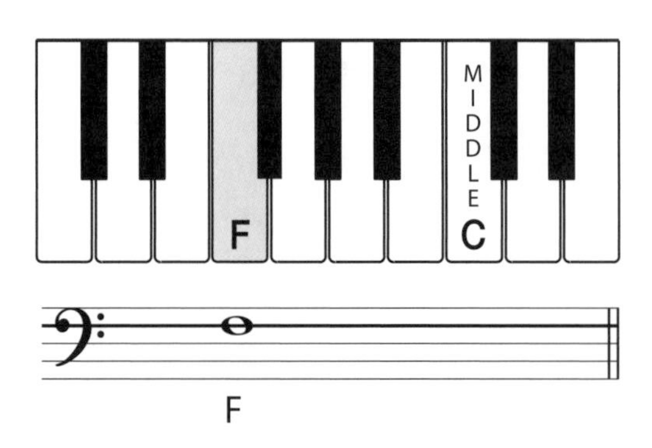

Some instruments that read bass clef include keyboard and percussion instruments, harp, trombone, tuba, bassoon, cello, double bass and bass guitar.

INTRODUCTION

The "grand staff" is made up of a treble clef staff on top and a bass clef staff below, joined together by a brace on the left side showing that both staves are to be played by one instrument. The grand staff is read by musicians who play keyboard instruments like piano and organ, as well as other instruments with a wide range such as marimba and harp.

There is a wide space between the treble staff and the bass staff to separate them visually from each other; believe it or not, this space makes it easier to read both clefs at once. Without it, the grand staff would look like one big eleven-line staff! Wouldn't that be confusing? As a result, although it looks like there is room for many notes between the staves, there is actually only one line between them; we call it "middle C."

When writing the note middle C, a *ledger line* is used to depict the line separating the treble and bass clef staves, which is usually invisible.

Despite what you see elsewhere on this page for illustration purposes, middle C is never actually placed in the exact middle of the grand staff in written music. If the right hand is playing middle C, it will appear just below the treble clef staff. If the left hand is playing middle C, it will appear right above the bass clef staff.

Follow middle C out in both directions and see why the notes are not the same in the two clefs, stopping when you get to the third line of each staff.

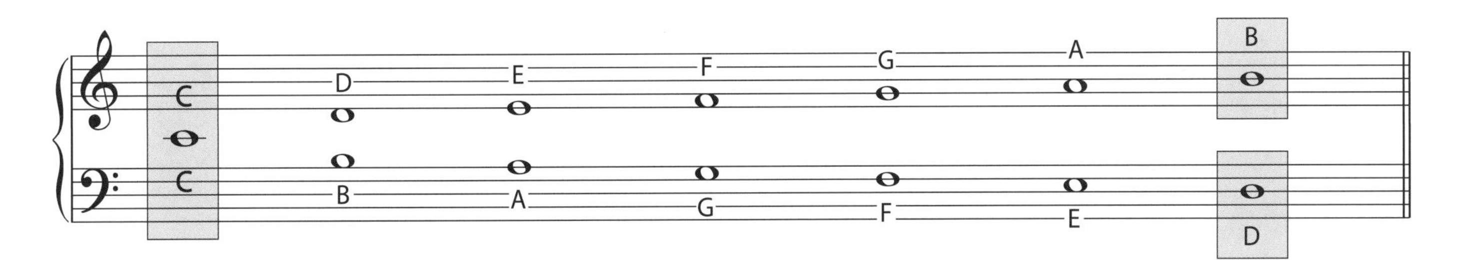

As you can see, line number three in the treble staff is B, while line number three in the bass staff is D. Now look at the image below: the two clefs of the grand staff work together to form one unbroken, repeating musical alphabet cycle from bottom to top. This is the reason the treble and bass clefs are read differently; each one is only half of the big picture!

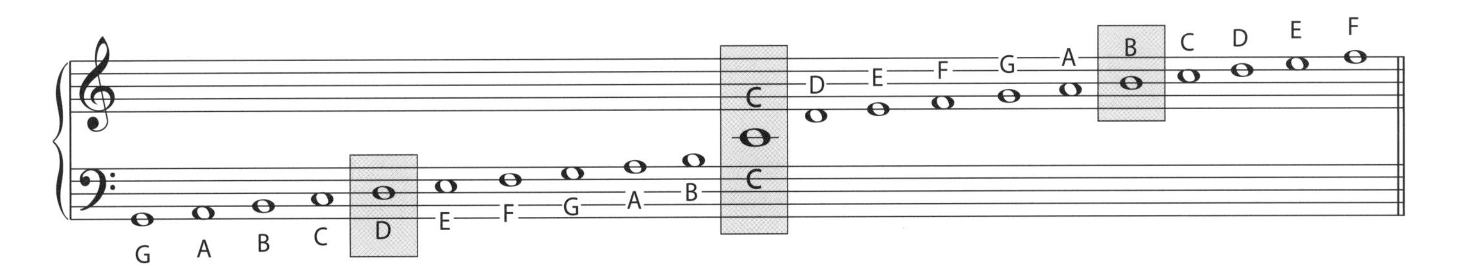

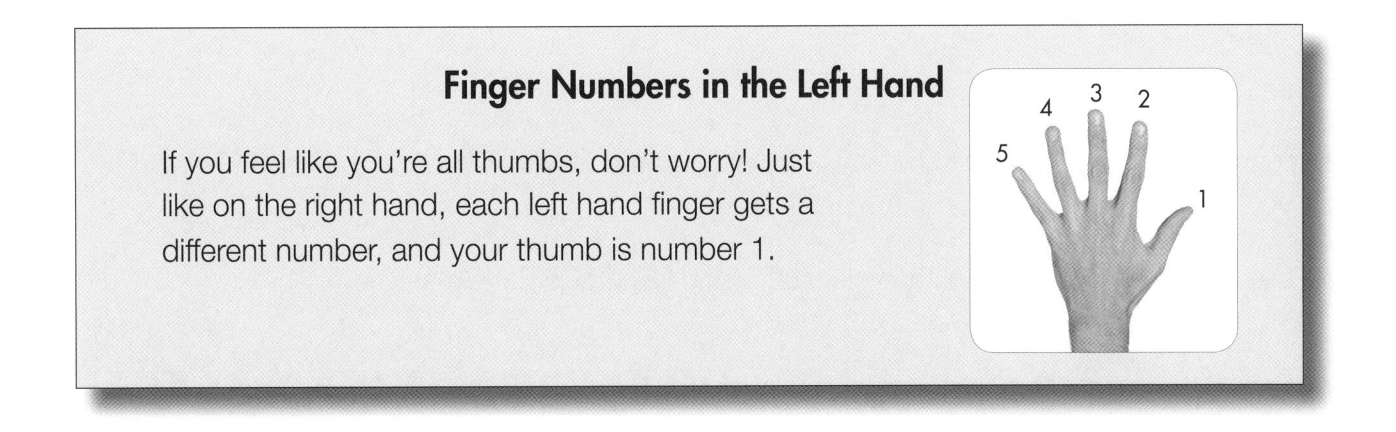

Finger Numbers in the Left Hand

If you feel like you're all thumbs, don't worry! Just like on the right hand, each left hand finger gets a different number, and your thumb is number 1.

In a five-finger position, your odd-numbered fingers are all on the same staff element: either all lines or all spaces. Your even-numbered fingers are on the opposite element: all spaces or all lines.

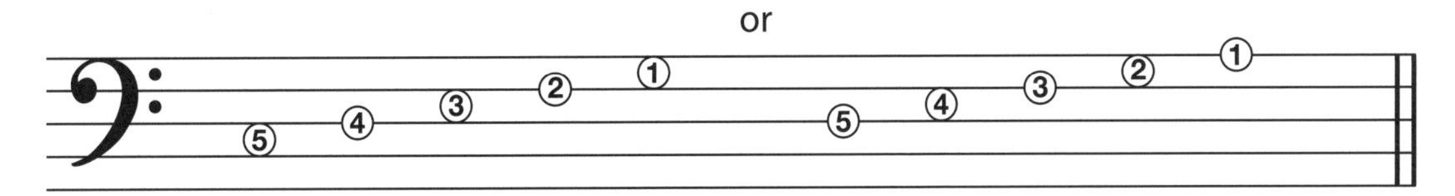

1 READING BASS C POSITION

- Learning Note Names from Bass Clef F
- Intervals: Unison, Second and Third
- Learning New Notes: Bass C and D
- Intervals: Fourth and Fifth
- Accompaniment Patterns
- Review

You've learned that the bass clef symbolizes the letter F, and indicates where the note F is on the staff. This is why the bass clef is sometimes called "F clef."

Circle the notes on the F line (the note on the fourth line from the bottom).

Another famous way to read the spaces in the bass clef is to use the sentence "All Cows Eat Grass," beginning from the bottom of the four spaces and reading up.

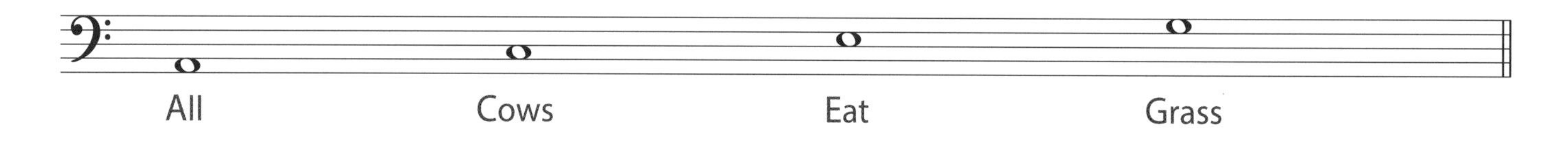

This mnemonic device works for the bass clef in the same way that spelling the word "F-A-C-E" helps you remember the spaces of the treble clef.

Label the following notes on the bass clef staff using "All Cows Eat Grass."

By filling in the line notes in between the space notes, you can see that as you ascend through the staff, the musical alphabet repeats.

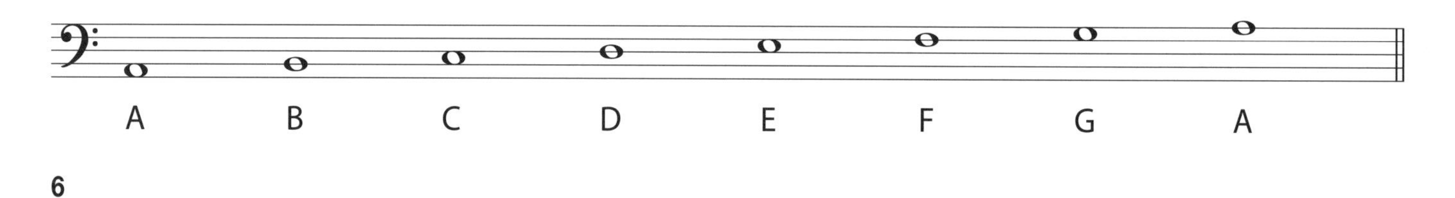

LEARNING NOTE NAMES FROM BASS CLEF F

Take another look at the F clef line. The notes that surround it are E (below F) and G (above F).

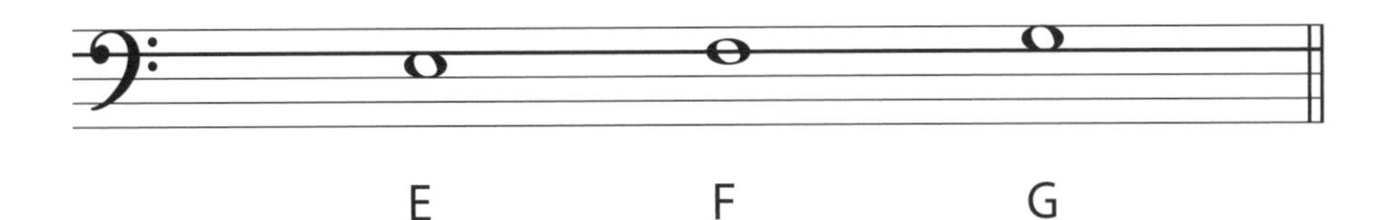

Draw these notes on the staff.

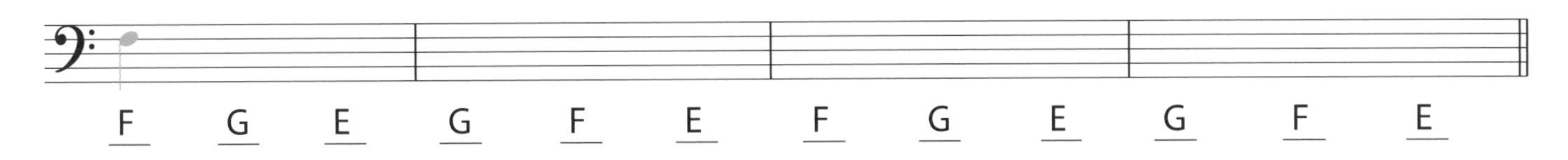

Practice these notes for fluency. Start with F and G. Say the note name as you play the exercise. Try using the provided fingering.

Now try E and F. Again, say the note name as you play each one.

CHALLENGE: Target Practice Game

For further fluency and speed in orienting your left hand to the bass clef staff, try this!

1. Choose an exercise from above.
2. Put your left hand behind your back.
3. Read and say the first note of the exercise.
4. Bring your left hand from behind your back, play the note, then put your hand behind your back again.
5. Repeat until you've finished the exercise.
6. When you're ready, time yourself!
   Write your best time here: _______ minutes _______ seconds

For an extra challenge, roll dice each time (with your right hand) to see which finger to use!

Now, you'll put the three notes together. Say and play each note.

INTERVALS: Unison, Second and Third

Intervals are used to measure and talk about the distance between two notes. They can either be played one at a time as in a "melody", or both at once as in a chord (also known as "harmony"). Unlike measuring with a ruler, when measuring intervals you count the first note. So for example, notes that are right next to each other are counted as two, and called a "second."

Melodic intervals are played one at a time:

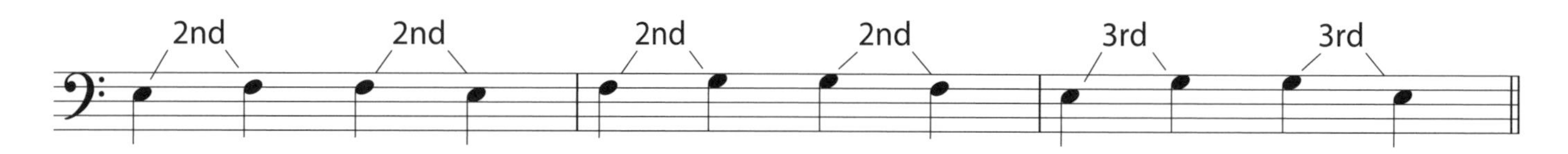

The interval is the same size whether the notes go up or down.

Harmonic intervals are played simultaneously:

As you can see, harmonic intervals share a stem. Seconds look strange, because they are so close together that they protrude out in different directions. This is because note heads can't overlap each other. As a side benefit, this helps you to spot them easily!

Thirds are also easy to see. They are always on two adjacent lines or two adjacent spaces. So far, you only know one third, the interval between E and G. These notes occupy two adjacent spaces.

A name for two adjacent notes on the same line or space is *unison*.

Major and Minor Seconds

The two most common types of seconds are minor seconds and major seconds. Minor seconds are one half step apart, and major seconds are two half steps (one whole step) apart. An example of a half step (minor second) is E to F, as there are no piano keys in between them. There is a whole step (major second) between F and G however, because there is one piano key between these notes.

Try these songs that use a combination of harmonic and melodic unisons, seconds and thirds.

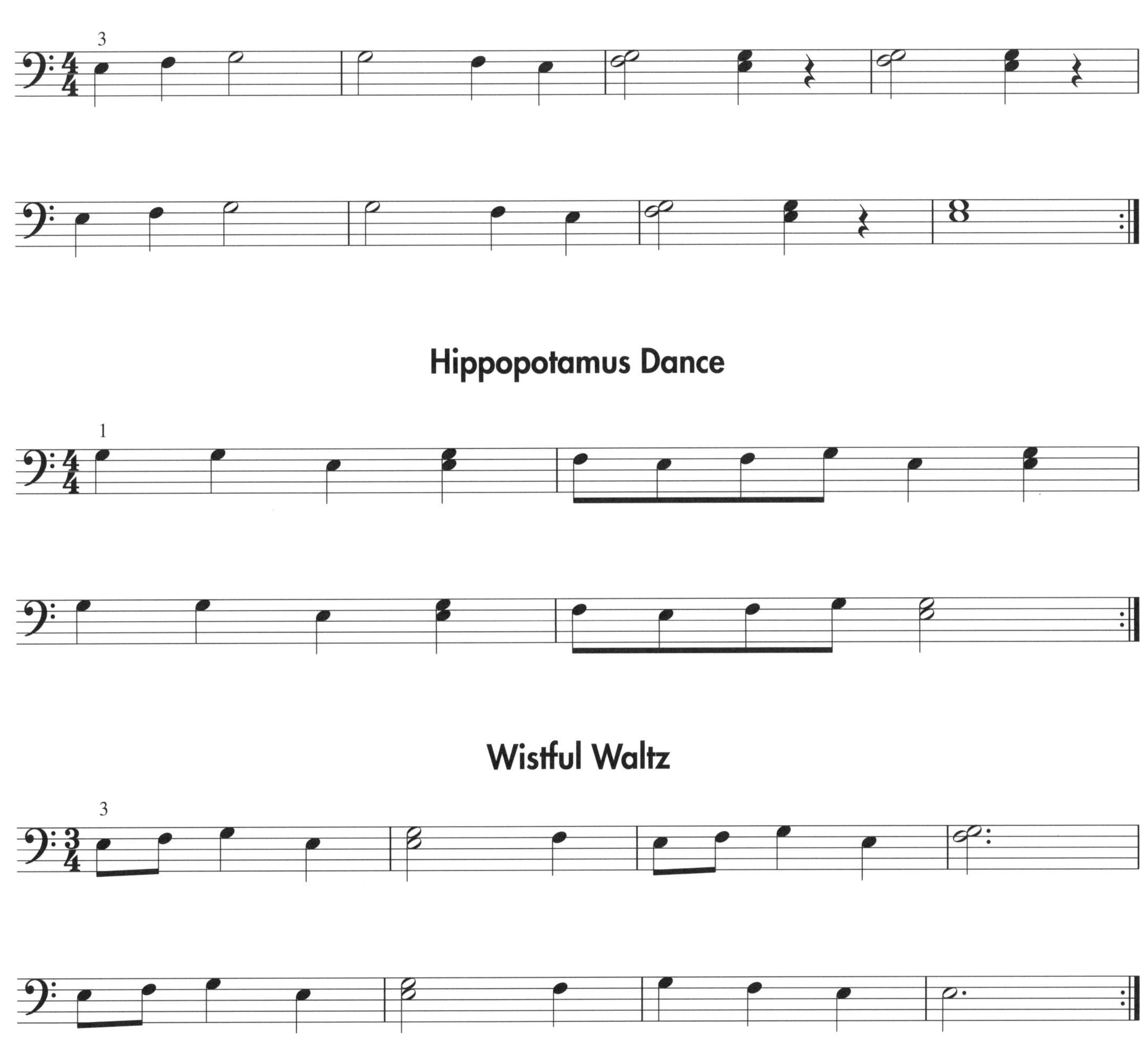

LEARNING NEW NOTES: Bass C and D

It's time to add some more notes: Bass C and D.

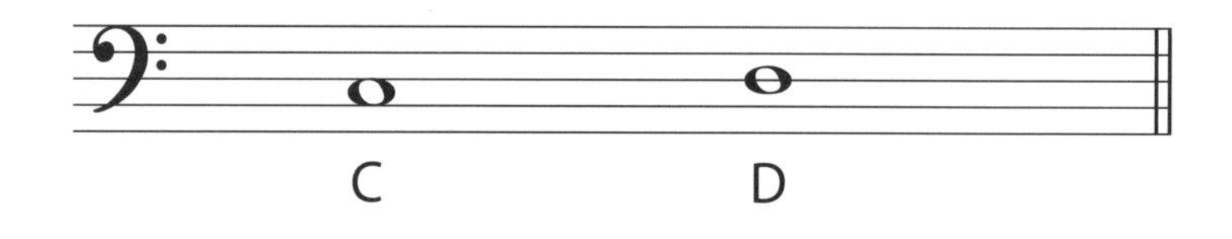

Draw a few Cs and Ds on the staff below. When writing notes with stems on the middle line or above, the stem should point down. Any notes below the middle line or lower, like your new Bass C, should be written with the stem pointing up.

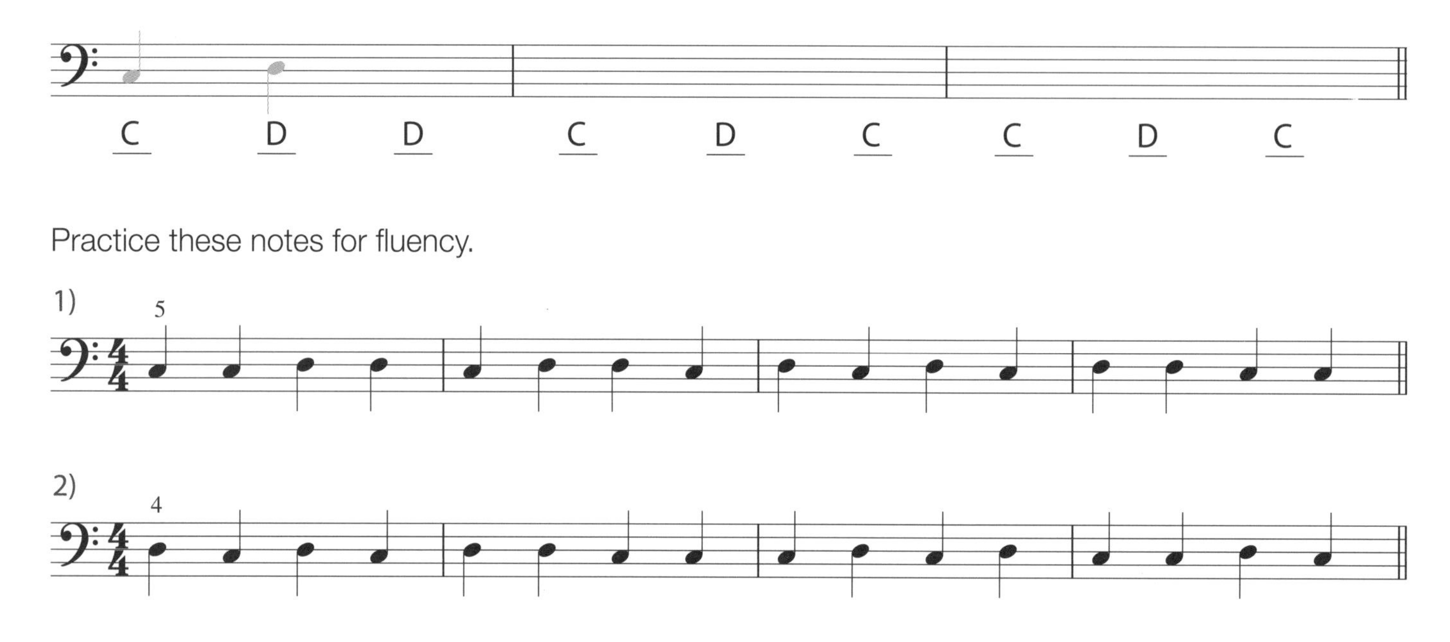

Practice these notes for fluency.

Now you have enough notes for a C major five-finger position. If you haven't done so already, go ahead and place your 5th finger on C, your 4th finger on D, and so forth.

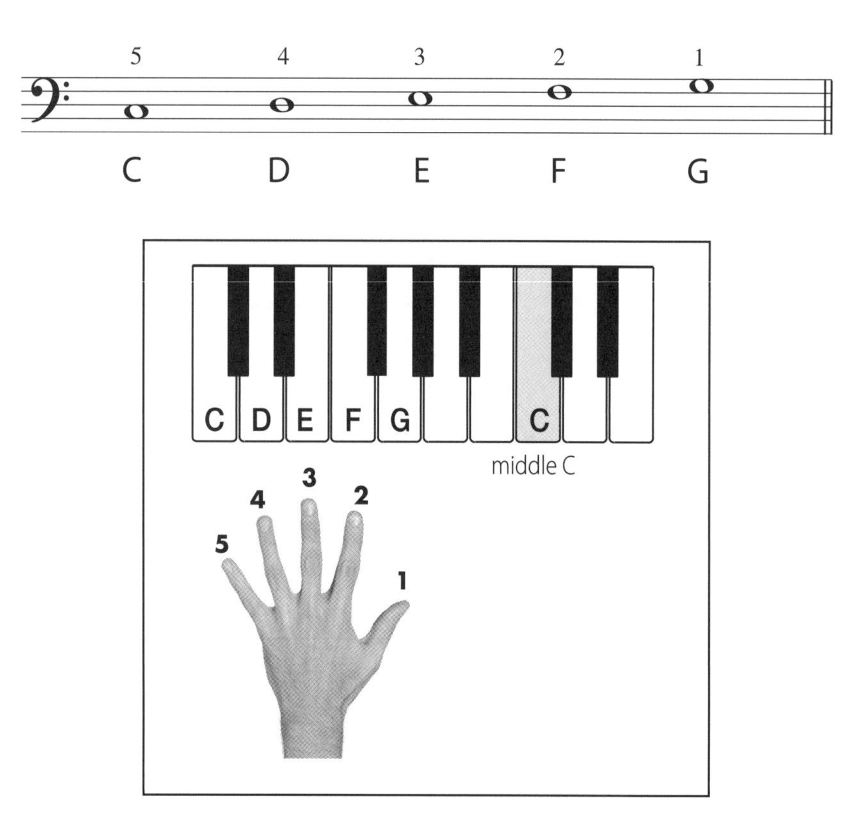

Use this position to play the following exercises. Name the intervals before playing.

Now use this position to play the following songs. Try to remember which finger belongs on each note without looking.

Mary Had a Little Lamb

INTERVALS: Fourth and Fifth

Let's learn two larger intervals: ***fourths*** and ***fifths***.

Count each line and space between each note (going up or down in pitch). Be sure to include the notes themselves.

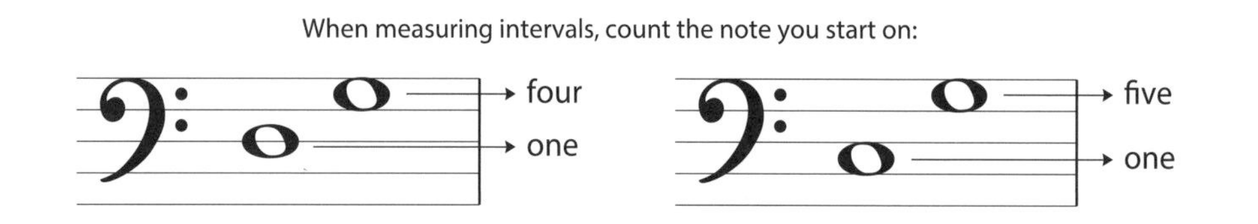

Play the following intervals using the C major five-finger pattern.

Melodic 4th and 5th Intervals

Harmonic 4th and 5th Intervals

You might start to see a pattern now: both notes of odd-numbered intervals will be on the same element of the staff; either both lines or both spaces. You might call them "two-of-a-kind!"

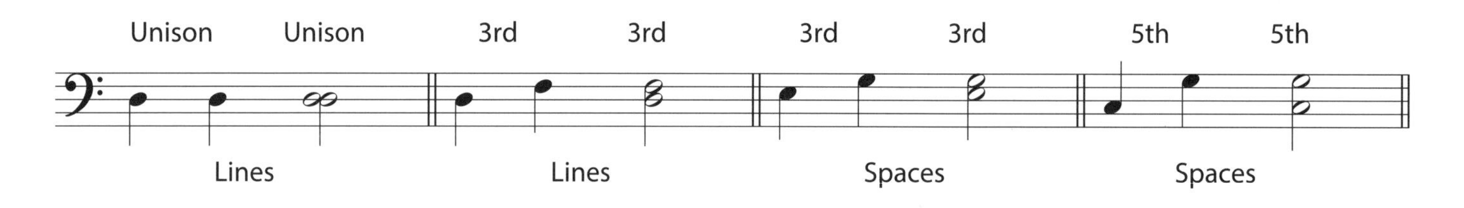

Of course, this means that even-numbered intervals are mixed; one note will be on a line, and the other on a space.

Name these intervals, then say and play these notes. Notice how fingers 1, 3 and 5 are on space notes, and fingers 2 and 4 are on line notes. This is because our odd-numbered fingers are a third apart from each other, making them three of a kind. The same is true for even-numbered fingers, but on the lines.

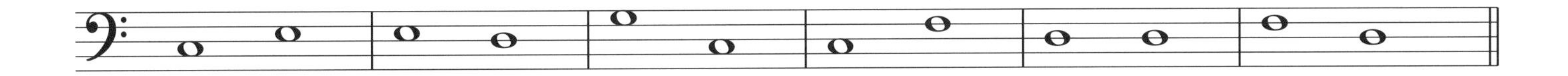

Write the intervals down from the G note. The first one is done for you.

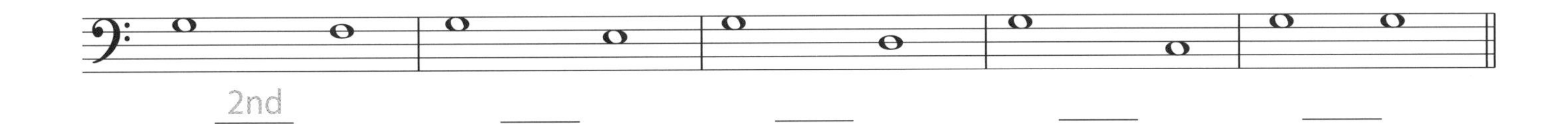

Draw the intervals indicated. The first one is done for you.

Creating Chords

A major function of the left hand is to provide harmonic reinforcement for a melody played in the right hand. This means you will often play chords in the left hand.

Chords are created by choosing a note (which is called a "root") and then stacking other notes in thirds on top. Here is what a C major chord looks like:

Notice that we've chosen the note C, and stacked two thirds on top, resulting in C, E and G. This is how you spell a C major chord.

Try playing a C major five-finger pattern and chord.

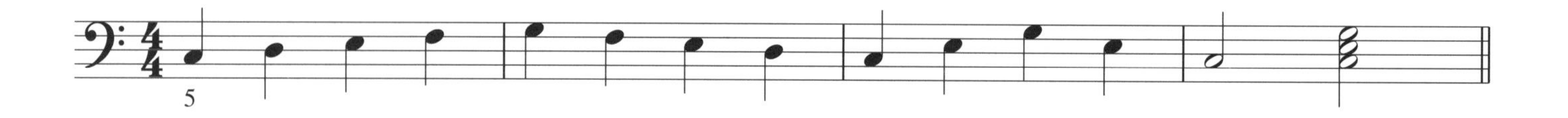

Some of these chords are C major chords, and some are not. Circle the C major chords and then play these three-note chords.

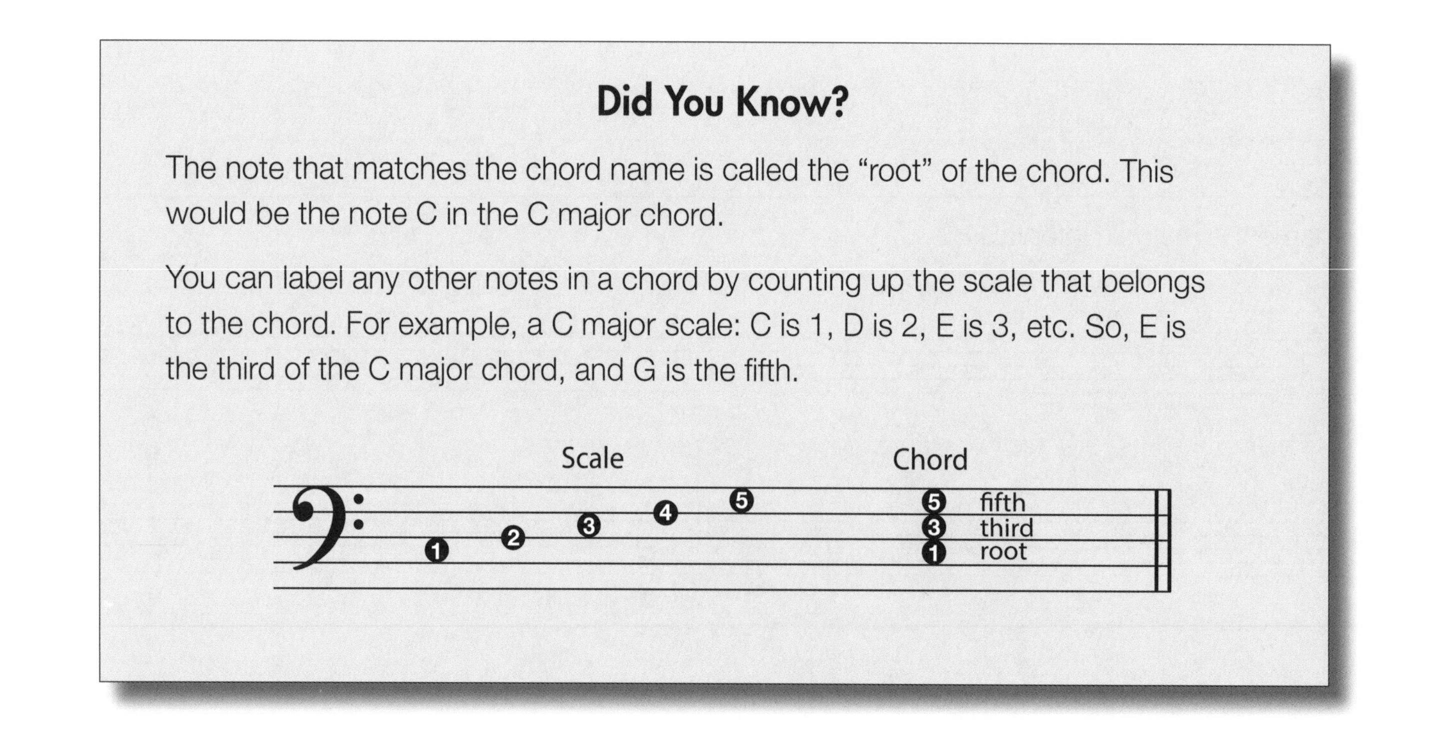

Did You Know?

The note that matches the chord name is called the "root" of the chord. This would be the note C in the C major chord.

You can label any other notes in a chord by counting up the scale that belongs to the chord. For example, a C major scale: C is 1, D is 2, E is 3, etc. So, E is the third of the C major chord, and G is the fifth.

ACCOMPANIMENT PATTERNS IN C

An almost endless variety of rhythms can be used in the left hand in order to accompany melodies in the right hand. Since this is the primary function of the left hand in piano playing, there is a short section of accompaniment patterns near the end of each chapter.

Here are some examples of patterns that use both melodic and harmonic intervals. Notice which notes belong to the C major chord (C, E or G) and which do not.

Here are more examples of accompaniment patterns that you will probably recognize from music you've heard or played before. You will find additions to this list throughout the book.

Waltz Time in C Major

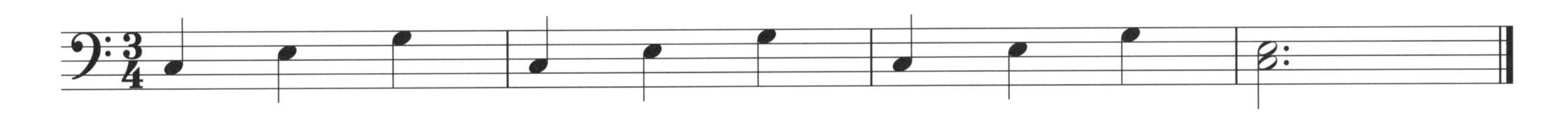

Alberti in C Major

Did You Know?

The "Alberti Bass" accompaniment pattern was named after Italian singer and composer Domenico Alberti, although he was neither the first nor the only composer to use patterns like these in his compositions. This pattern in particular became extremely popular during the Classical period, and was used by Haydn, Mozart and Beethoven, to name just a few!

CHALLENGE: Advanced Rhythm

Now you are ready to try some more complicated accompaniment patterns. You may find it helpful to count and clap the rhythm before you play. Don't forget that a tie (the little arc connecting two notes) works like glue to create one note out of two. Give it a try!

REVIEW

Here are more songs using just the bass clef notes you know so far. Enjoy using your new knowledge!

Lightly Row

Liza Jane

Drink to Me Only with Thine Eyes

When the Saints Go Marching In

CHAPTER 2

READING G POSITION

- Learning Note Names from G to E Above Middle C
- Intervals: Sixth, Seventh and Octave
- Songs Using New Notes
- Accidentals: Introducing F♯
- Accompaniment Patterns in G
- Review

LEARNING NEW NOTES FROM G TO E ABOVE MIDDLE C

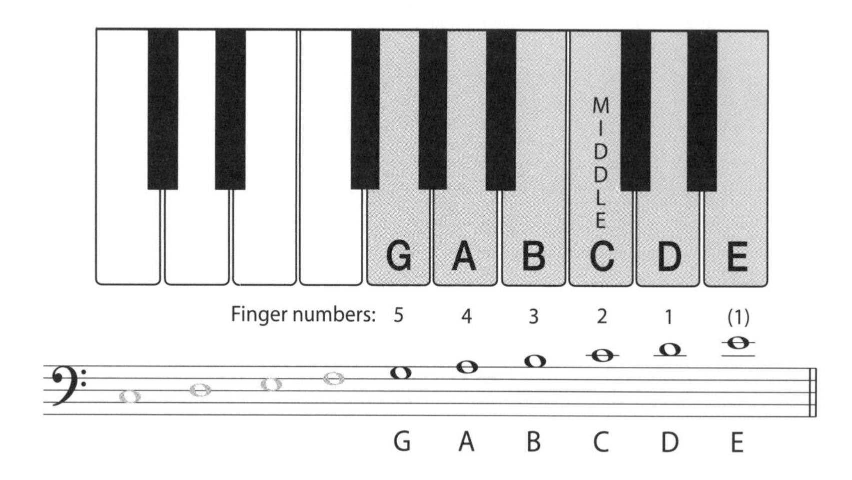

Remember the note G from Chapter 1. Now use it as the basis for a new hand position. Although only three notes are introduced at a time, use the notated fingerings in each exercise in order to strengthen fingers 3, 4 and 5.

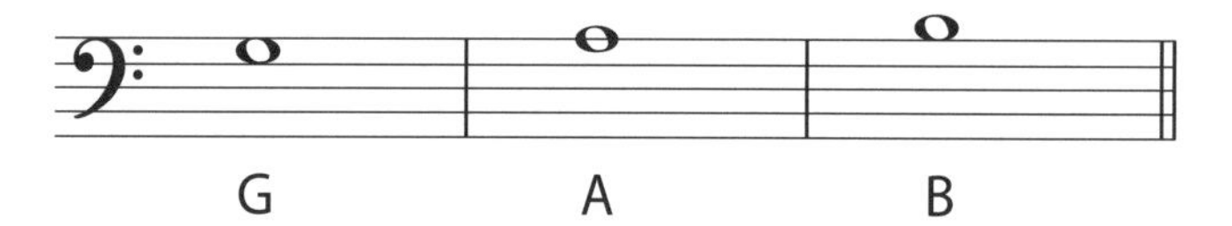

Draw these notes on the staff.

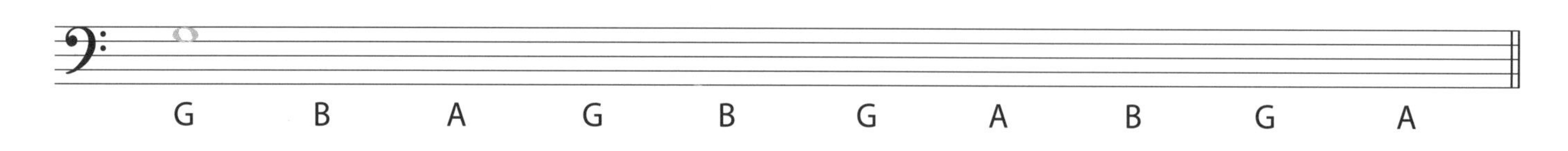

Practice these notes for fluency, starting with G and A. As always, say the note name as you play the exercise.

Now give A and B a try.

This time, you'll put them all together.

Draw a note to create the melodic interval indicated, then write the name of the note you drew. As a reminder, melodic means one note at a time, as in a melody.

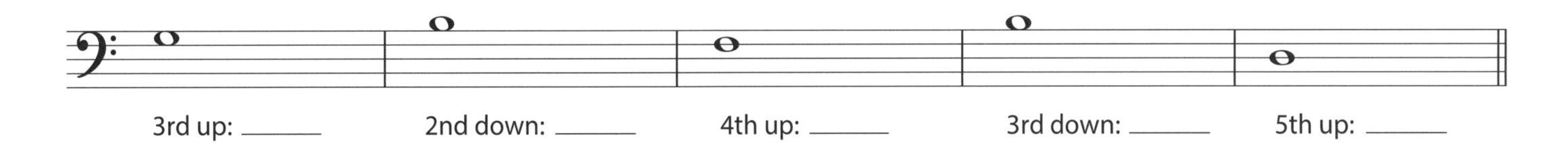

Learn these three new notes: middle C, D and E.

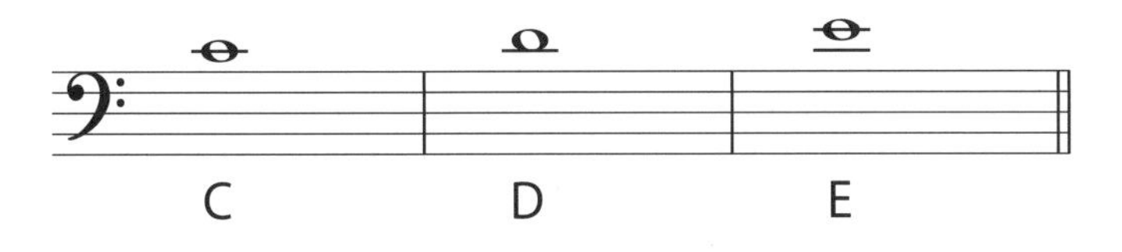

These notes are special, as they are also found in the treble clef more often than any of the other notes you will cover in this book. However, they still occur regularly in bass clef, so they'll be a main focus of this chapter.

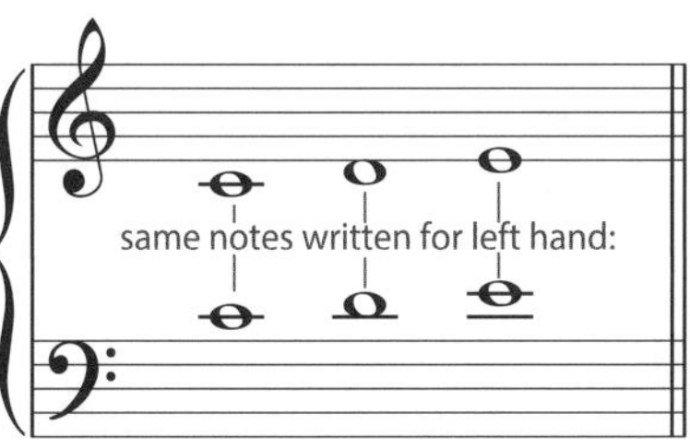

Here are middle C, D and E in both treble and bass clef:

Remember, middle C is called middle C because it is found in both the middle of the grand staff and the middle of the piano keyboard. It is written with one *ledger line* going through the middle of the note head. Any notes higher than middle C in the bass clef will also be written using ledger lines.

Draw these notes on the staff. Remember, middle C and E are still line notes, and D is a space note, even though you're using ledger lines.

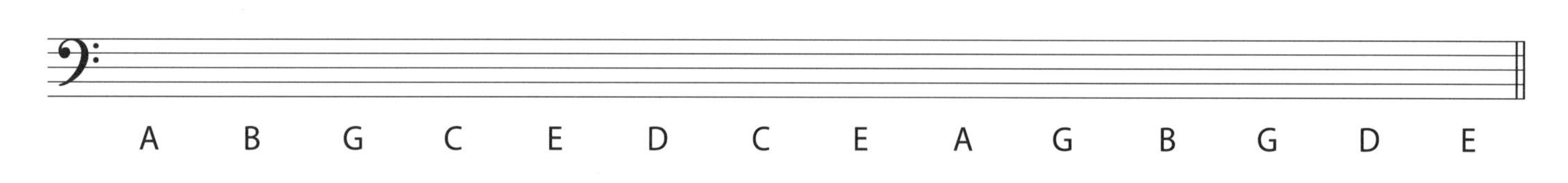

Practice reading middle C and D; say and play the notes.

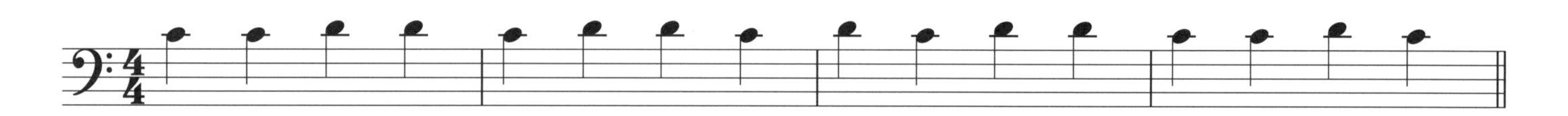

Now try D and E above middle C; say and play the notes.

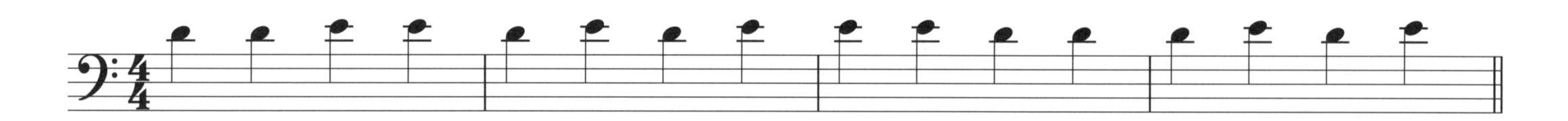

Sometimes it can be difficult to tell middle C and E apart. Practice just those two notes.

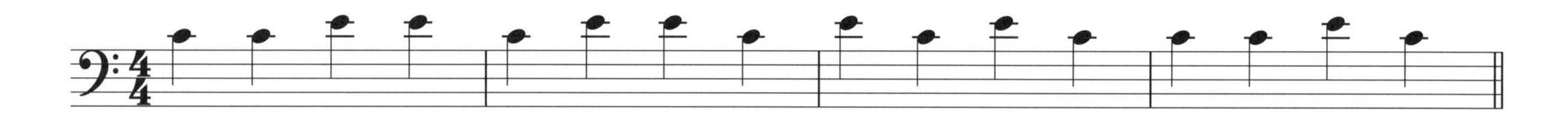

Now put all three together.

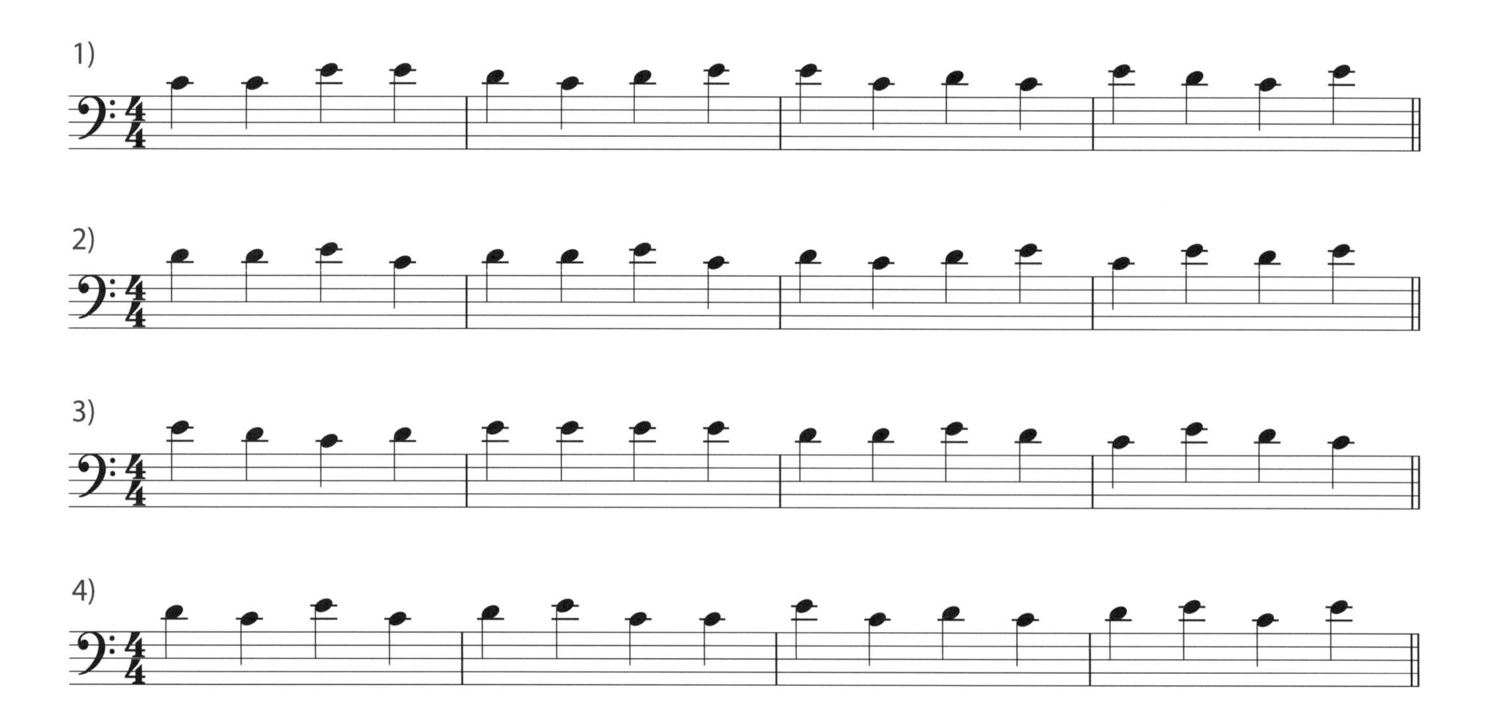

INTERVALS: Sixth, Seventh and Octave

The largest interval you learned in Chapter 1 was a fifth. Now that you have more notes to work with, learn to identify and play sixths, sevenths and octaves. Recognizing intervals is a very important part of reading and playing music, which is why they are emphasized in this book.

When reading the interval of a sixth, it can be helpful to be able to spot a fifth quickly. This allows you to simply move up one more note to find a sixth.

Here is the simplest way to spot a fifth:

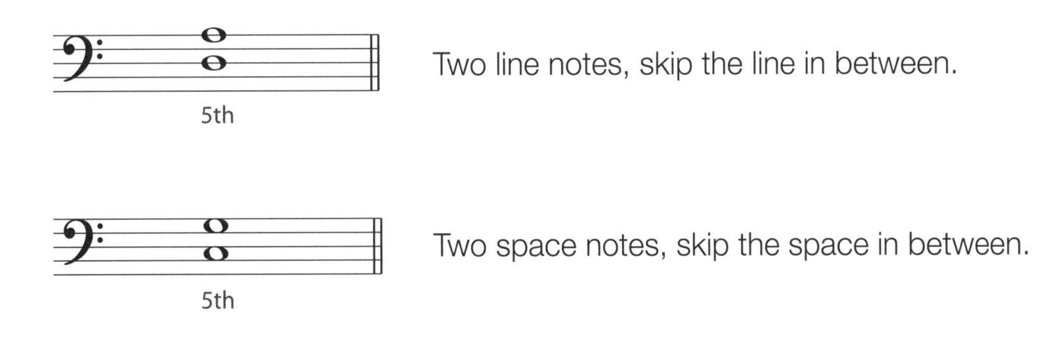

The interval of a sixth is one note larger than a fifth. Identify the intervals below.

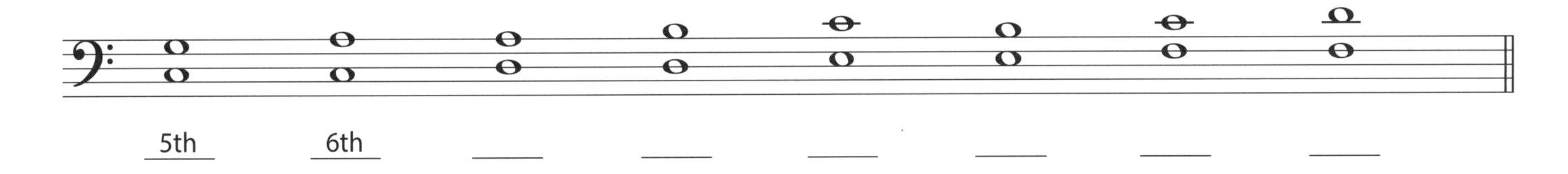

Skip a line or space to spot the fifth, then move out one line or space further to draw a harmonic sixth above or below as indicated.

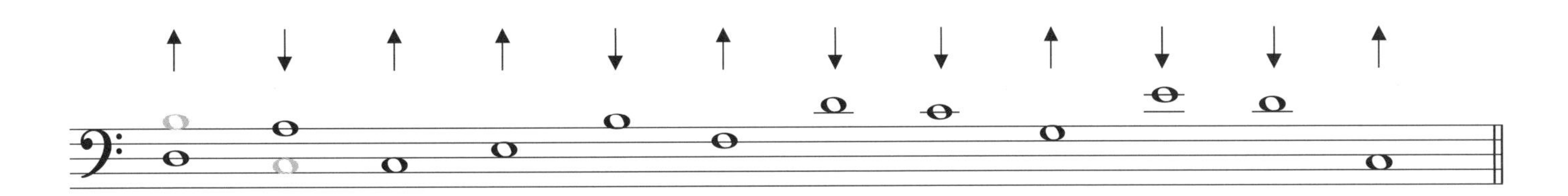

You've already learned that odd-numbered intervals are two of a kind, in that they are either both on lines or both on spaces. Even-numbered intervals are mixed; one note on a line and one on a space. Your new interval of a seventh is two of a kind.

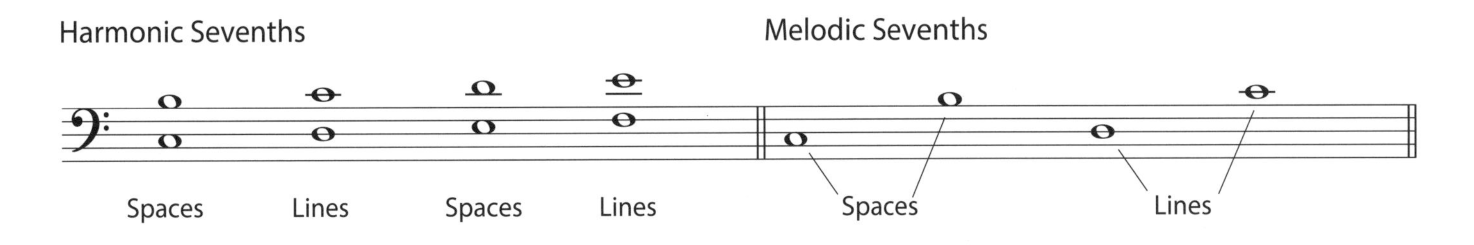

Draw harmonic sevenths below, and make sure to match lines or spaces with the given note. Skip two lines or two spaces in between.

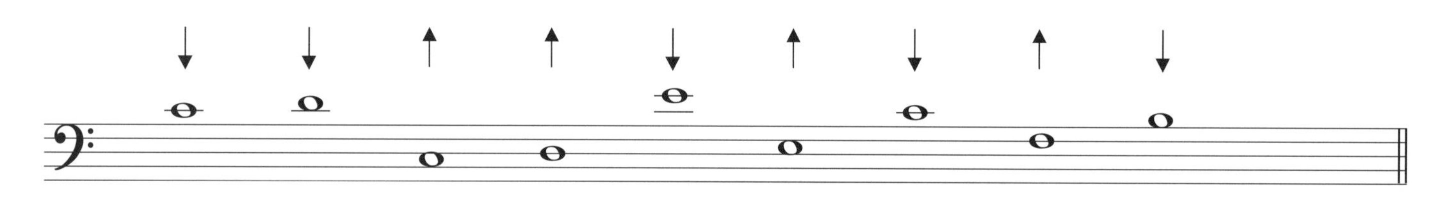

The interval of an eighth is so important in music that it gets its own name: *octave*. This word comes from the Latin word "octo," meaning eight.

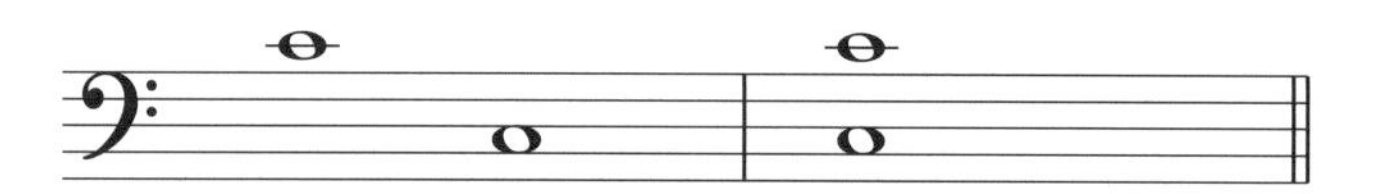

Draw harmonic octaves below.

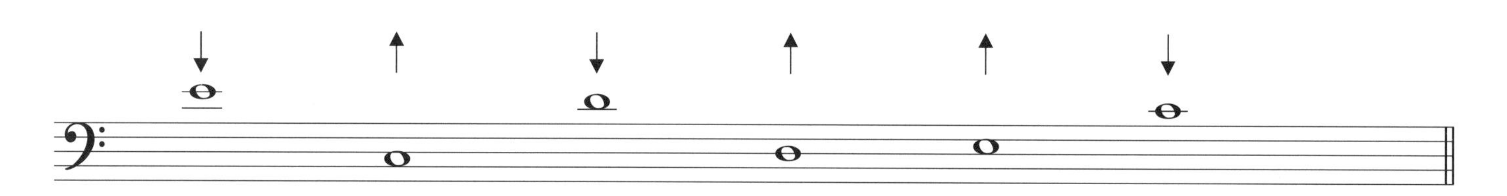

Practice all the intervals you know so far by naming the interval between each note.

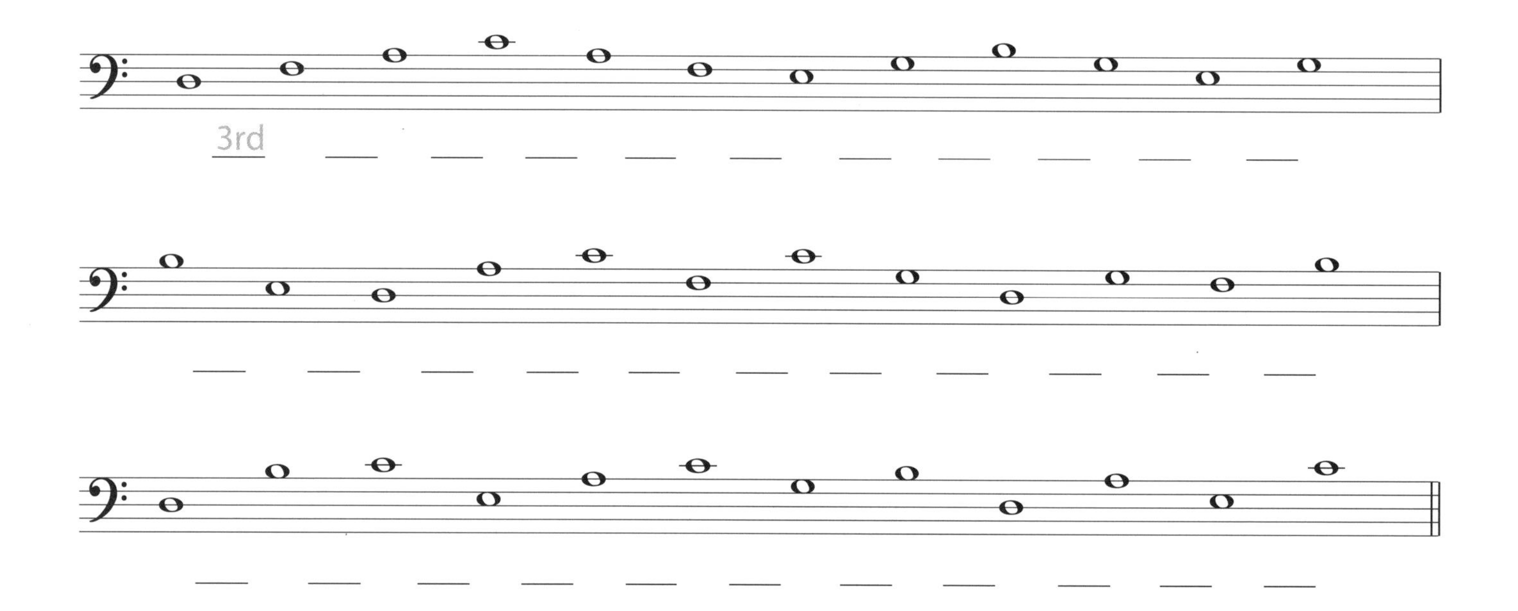

SONGS USING NEW NOTES

On the next page are songs using the notes from the top space G through E above middle C.

In the selection, "Spring," by Vivaldi, you'll see that one of the finger numbers has a circle around it. A circled finger number means that you'll be changing your hand position.

Sad Mary

Notice the "2 x 1" in the last line of the song. This indicates that finger 1 will cross under finger 2 to get to the C, then end up in a new location with finger 1 on C to continue the piece.

ACCIDENTALS: INTRODUCING F♯

Chapter 1 is in the key of C, which has no sharps or flats. To play songs and accompaniment patterns in G major, it's time to learn F sharp (F♯). A sharp raises the note by one half step.

The way to cancel out a sharp or a flat is with the natural symbol (♮):

Say and play these notes. Remember that accidentals carry over only to the end of the measure.

ACCOMPANIMENT PATTERNS IN G

Try these accompaniment patterns in G major.

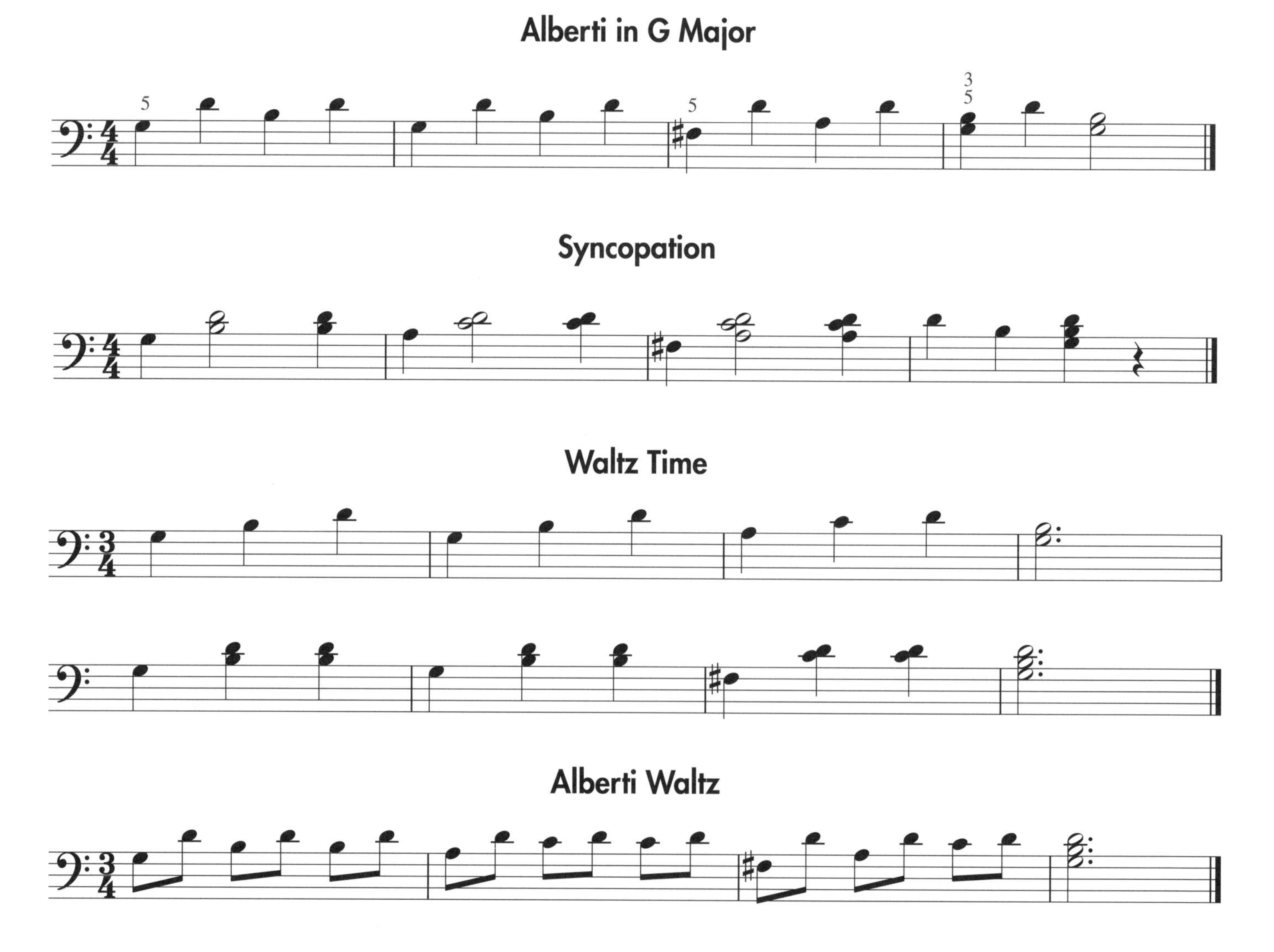

Creating Chords

Chapter 1 taught that one way a chord is built is by stacking notes in thirds on top of a note called the "root" (the note that shares the letter name of the chord.) Now that you have become familiar with more notes, create more chords this way.

Draw thirds on top of the given root note. Remember, they are "three of a kind."

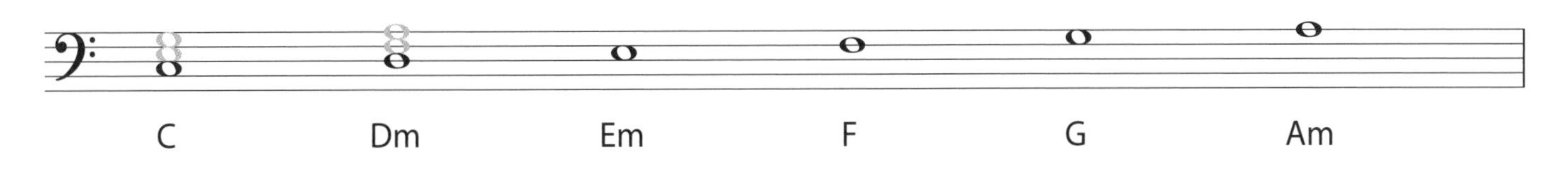

Did you notice the lowercase "m"s after some of the letters? Symbols like this are used to show the chord's quality; that is, whether a chord is major, minor, or something else. The lowercase "m" indicates *minor*. If there is no symbol, the chord is major.

Circle the major chords above; these are the chords that have no symbols other than the letter name of their root. There are three: C, F and G.

Play these major chords and notice they have a "happy" or "bright" sound. Use finger 5 for the root, finger 3 for the third and finger 1 for the fifth.

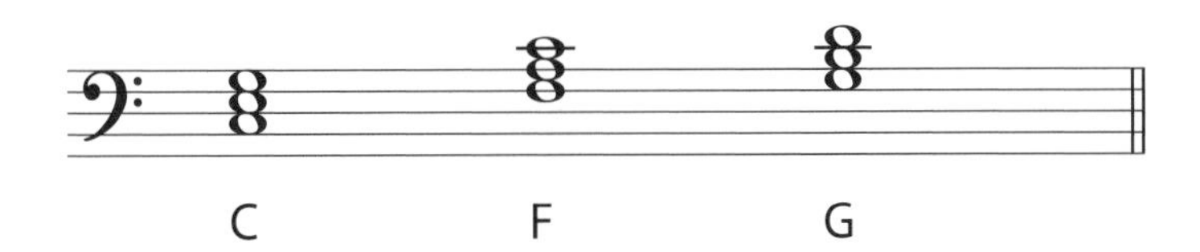

Now, play these minor chords and notice they have a "sad" or "dark" sound, compared to the major chords above. Use the same fingering for these chords as for the major chords.

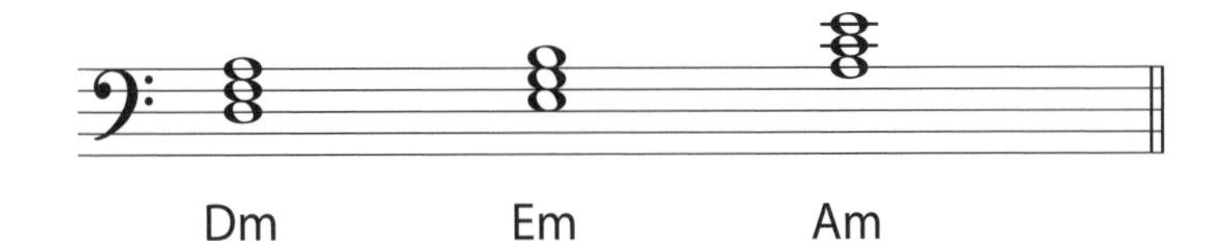

Take a look back at the accompaniment patterns on the previous page. Did you notice some of the same groups of notes that you used to create chords? For example, the notes G, B and D are often used together, because they spell a G major chord.

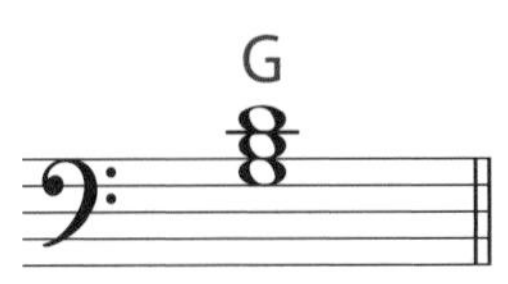

Accompaniment patterns are created by playing notes from chords using different rhythms. Here are examples of the G major chord as it is used in different ways on page 24.

Chords are used in this way throughout the book to create many different accompaniment patterns.

REVIEW

To review the notes you've learned so far: Draw the notes that spell these words. You now have two choices for the notes C, D and E; it's up to you which octave to choose.

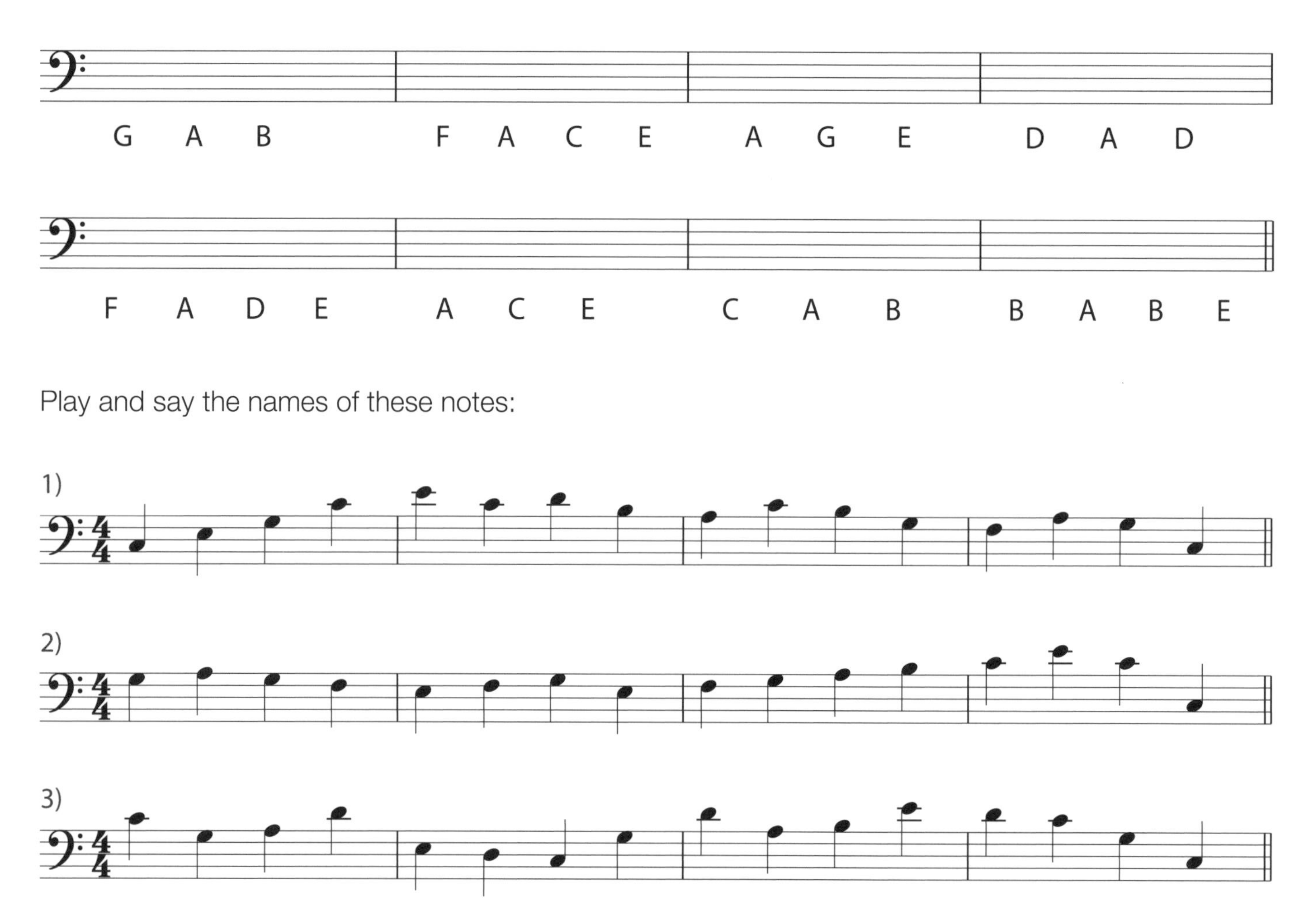

Play and say the names of these notes:

You are nearing the end of Chapter 2, and have now been introduced to ten bass clef notes (eleven if you count F♯.) We will continue to suggest fingerings for you, but with this many notes, it's harder to stay in one hand position. Since the purpose of this book is to teach you to read notes rather than fingerings, feel free to use whatever fingering works for you.

Enjoy these songs using all the notes you've learned so far.

Row Your Boat

Skip to My Lou

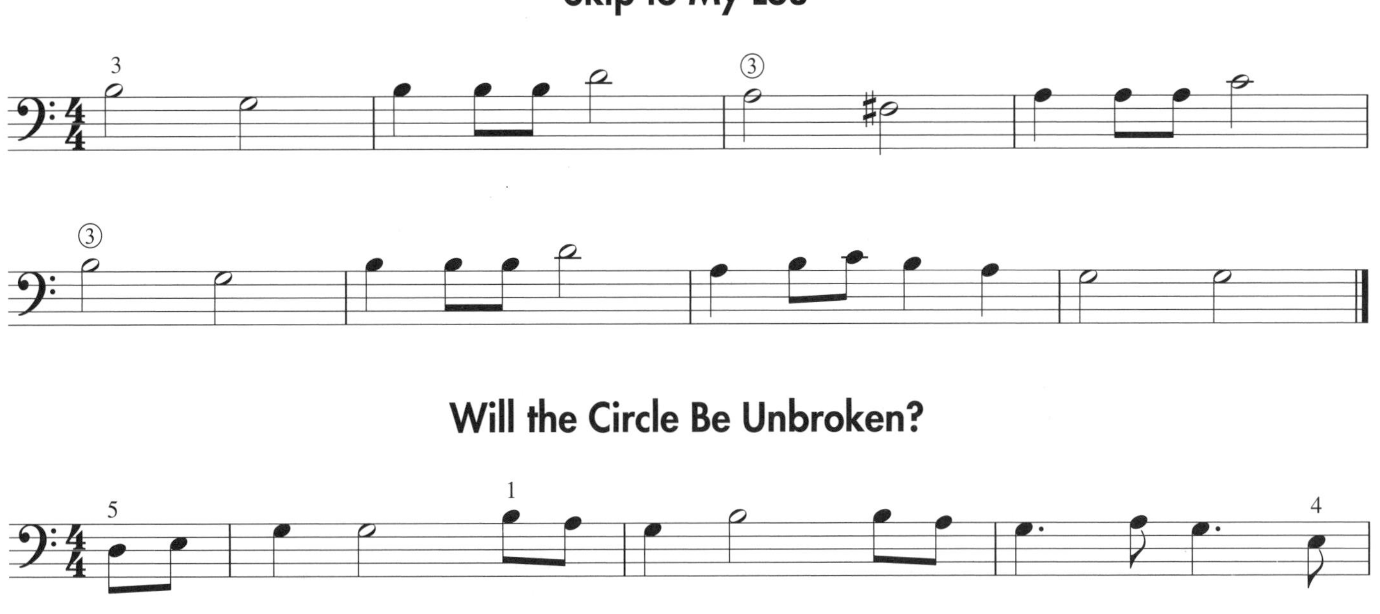

Will the Circle Be Unbroken?

Taps

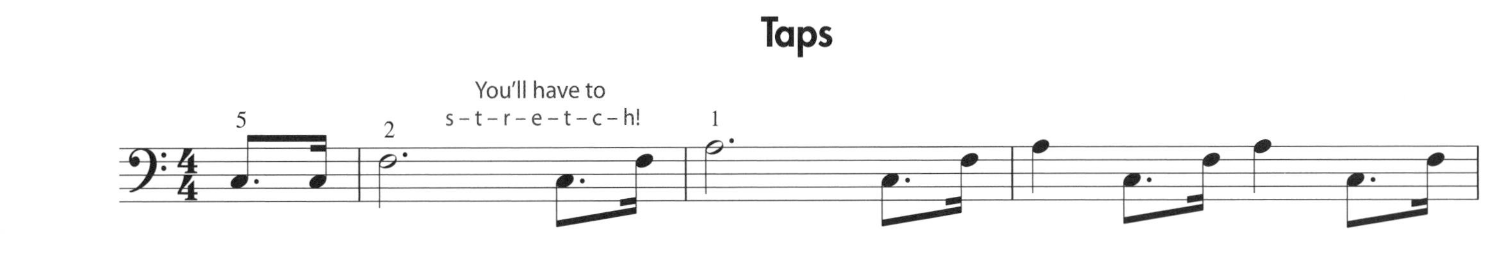

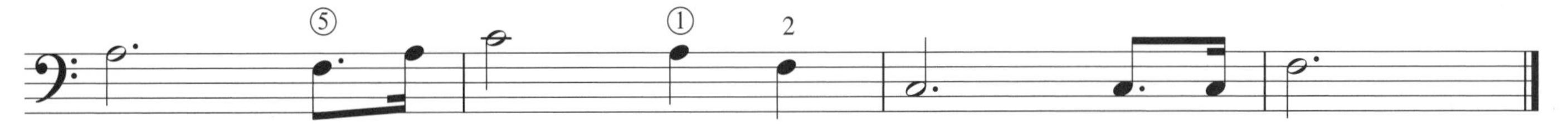

Eine Kleine Nachtmusik

Wolfgang Amadeus Mozart

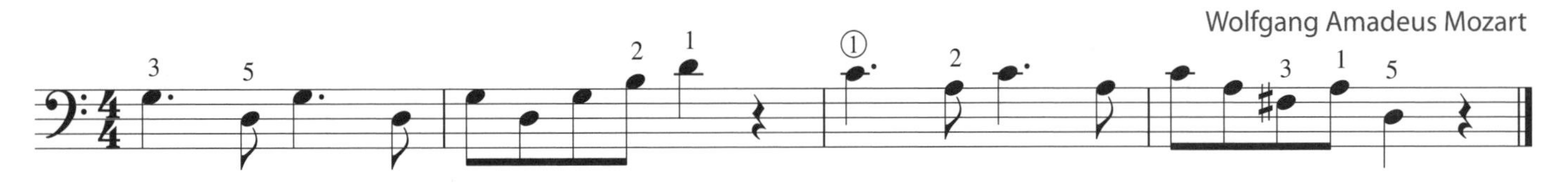

Theme from *Swan Lake*

Pyotr Ilyich Tchaikovsky

CHALLENGE: More Accidentals

Play this song, which contains other accidentals than the one we've discussed so far. Remember, a sharp means go up to the very next note. A natural cancels out a sharp. Try to figure this song out.

Midnight Special

CHALLENGE: Two Hands in Bass Clef

In Chapter 1 you learned "When the Saints Go Marching In." Try this version for both hands in bass clef.

When the Saints Go Marching In

READING LOW F POSITION

- Learning Note Names from Low F to Low B
- Accidentals: Introducing B♭
- Songs Using New Notes
- Accompaniment Patterns
- Review

LEARNING NOTE NAMES FROM LOW F TO LOW B

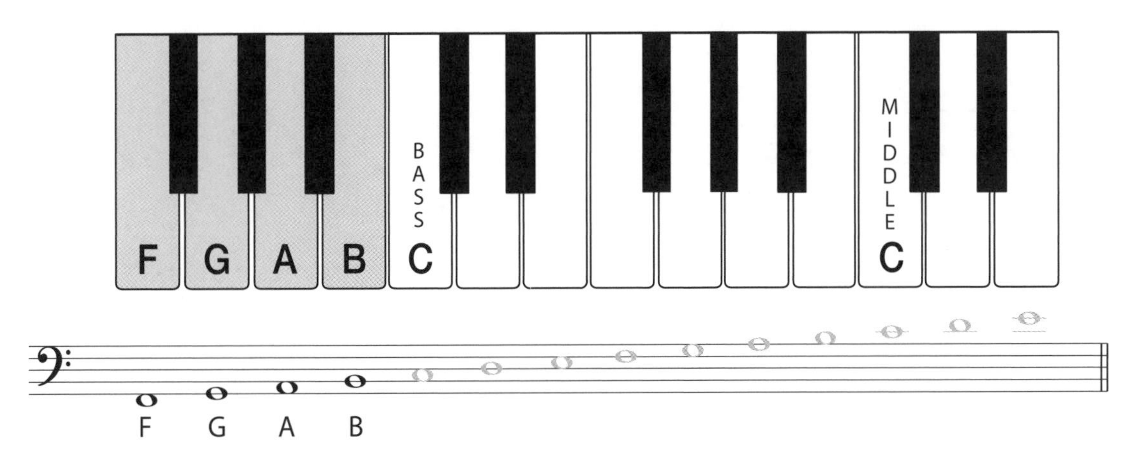

You remember the note Bass C from Chapter 1; now you're going to learn the four notes below it on the bass clef staff, starting just below the bottom staff line.

Draw these new notes on the staff.

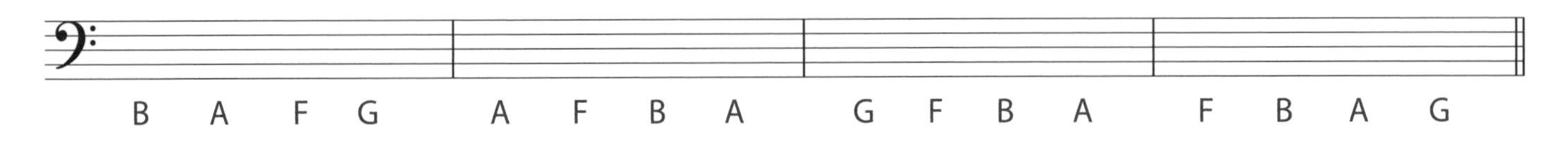

Practice these notes for fluency, starting with A and B. As always, say the note name as you play the exercise.

Now give F and G a try.

Sometimes it can be difficult to tell "two of a kind" notes apart—try just F and A.

Now try just G and B.

Finally, put them all together.

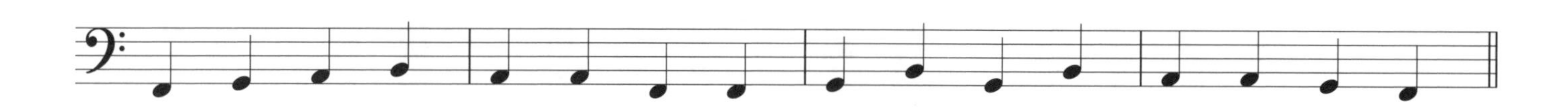

Draw a note to create the harmonic interval indicated, then write the name of the note you drew. As a reminder, harmonic means more than one note at a time, as in a chord.

ACCIDENTALS: Introducing B♭

In Chapter 2, you were introduced to the concepts of sharp and natural symbols and their effect on notes. A flat lowers the note by one half step. B♭ looks like this:

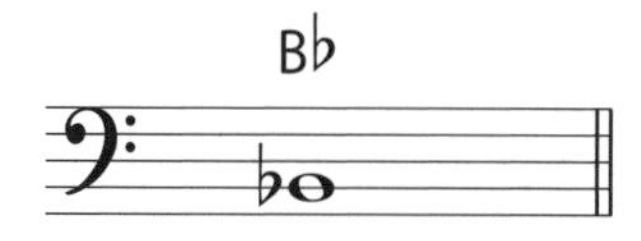

The way to cancel out a flat is the natural (♮) symbol; it works for canceling out either a sharp or a flat.

Say and play these notes. Remember that accidentals carry throughout the bar.

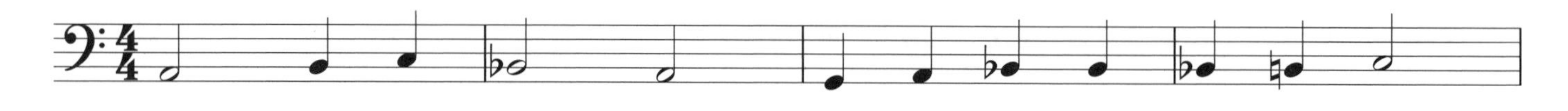

SONGS USING NEW NOTES

These songs include your new notes as well as some notes from previous chapters.

ACCOMPANIMENT PATTERNS

The following songs are in the keys of C, F and G major.

* Note that the flat symbol applies to B, not to C.

Chord Inversions

Chapter 2 introduced forming chords by stacking thirds on top of the root of the chord. For example, the note C is the root note of a C major chord, and the other two notes are E (the third) and G (the fifth.) However, it's important to know that this is not the only shape a chord can come in. You can change the octaves of any of the notes; as long as the chord still contains C, E and G, it's still a C major chord. The new shape is an *inversion*.

- A chord with the root on the bottom is in "root position."
- A chord with the third on the bottom is in the "first inversion."
- A chord with the fifth on the bottom is in the "second inversion."

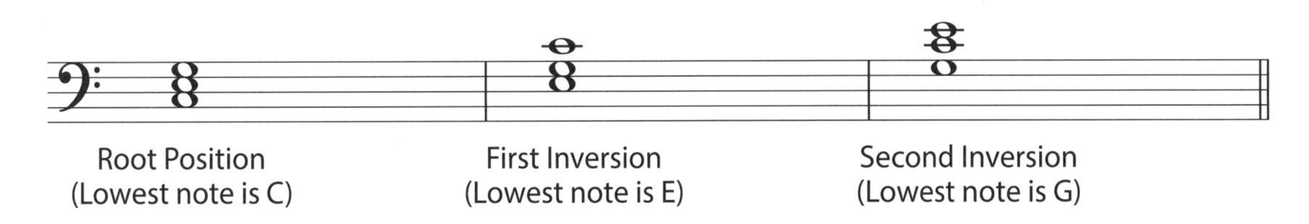

In each chord, the notes are C, E and G—they are just in a different order. Now look at the intervals made by each chord. As you can see:

- A root position chord is made by stacking two thirds on top of each other.
- A first inversion chord has a third on the bottom and a fourth on the top.
- A second inversion chord is the opposite: a fourth on the bottom, and a third on the top.

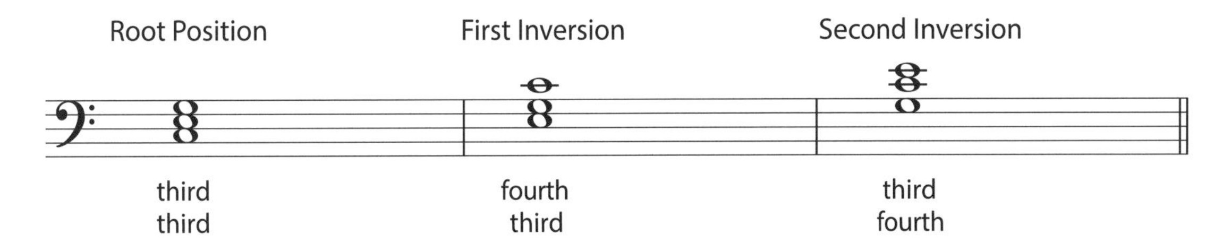

Below are chords in root position, first inversion and second inversion. Use the intervals to spot the inversion. Under each chord, write "R" if the chord is in root position, "1" if the chord is in first inversion, or "2" if the chord is in second inversion.

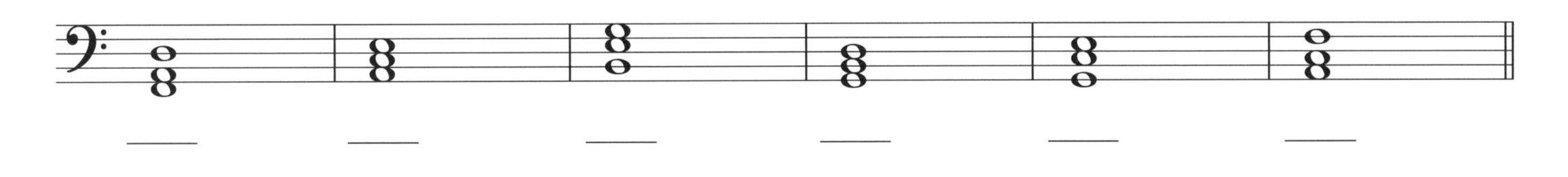

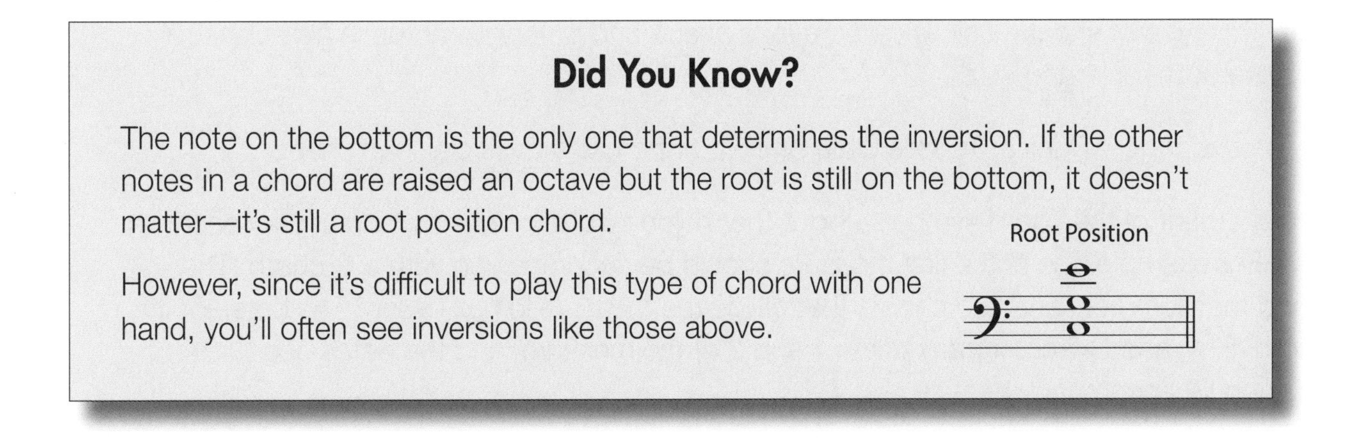

Did You Know?

The note on the bottom is the only one that determines the inversion. If the other notes in a chord are raised an octave but the root is still on the bottom, it doesn't matter—it's still a root position chord.

However, since it's difficult to play this type of chord with one hand, you'll often see inversions like those above.

Chords and Accompaniment

Here are variations on playing a common chord progression. Notice that a note can be omitted from each chord and though the sound is different, the chord progression is still recognizable.

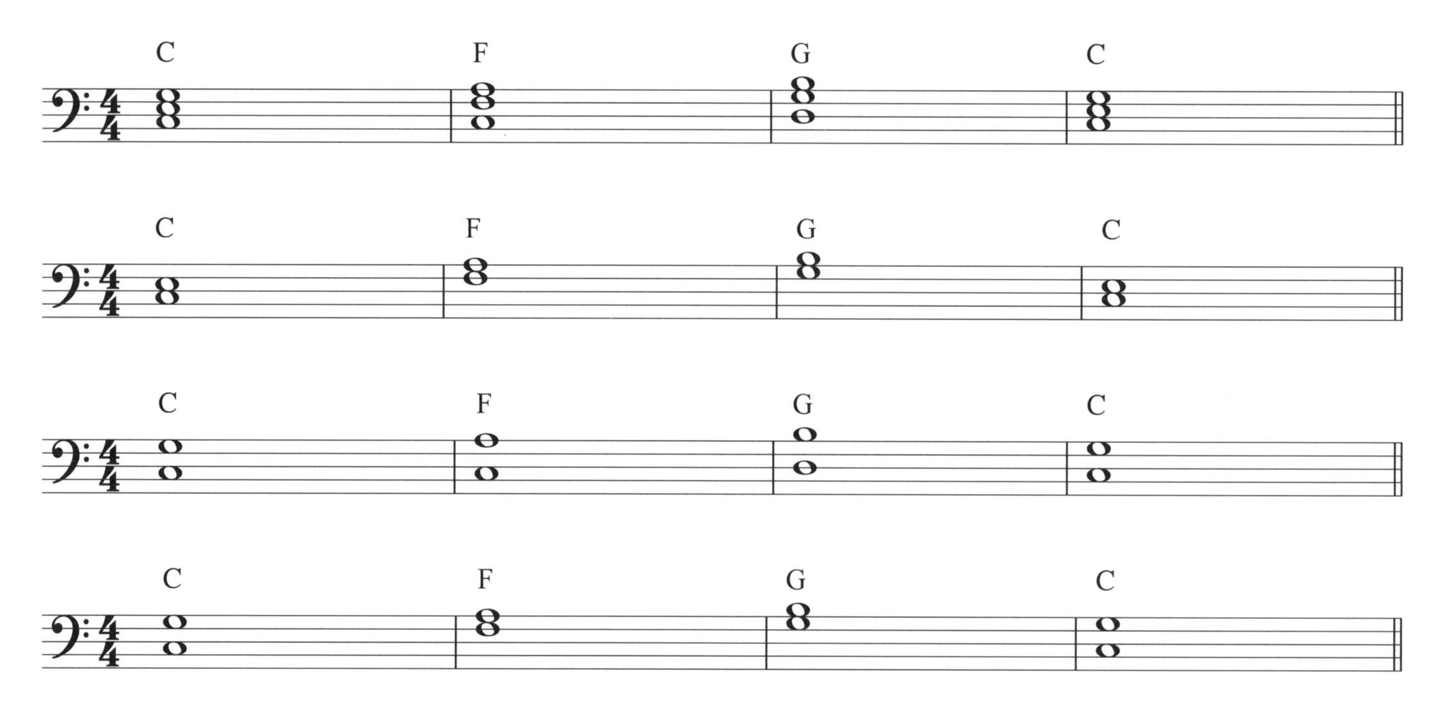

The chords above are called *block chords*, because all the notes of the chord are played at once. When the notes of a chord are played one at a time, these are called *broken chords*. Try the chord progression again, this time in two different broken chord styles.

Pianists don't always play music written on the grand staff. As you advance, you will encounter music written as just a melody (usually in treble clef) with chord symbols above the notes. This type of sheet music is called a *lead sheet*, and is very common in non-classical styles like pop, rock, and jazz.

On the next page, "Twinkle, Twinkle Little Star" is written as a bass clef lead sheet.

The placement of the chord symbols above the melody will tell you how long to play each chord. For example, the entire first measure should be accompanied with a C chord. The second measure contains two chords that divide the measure in half evenly. The notes of an F chord (F, A, and C) accompany beats 1 and 2 of the measure, and the notes of a C chord (C, E, and G) accompany beats 3 and 4.

Twinkle, Twinkle Little Star

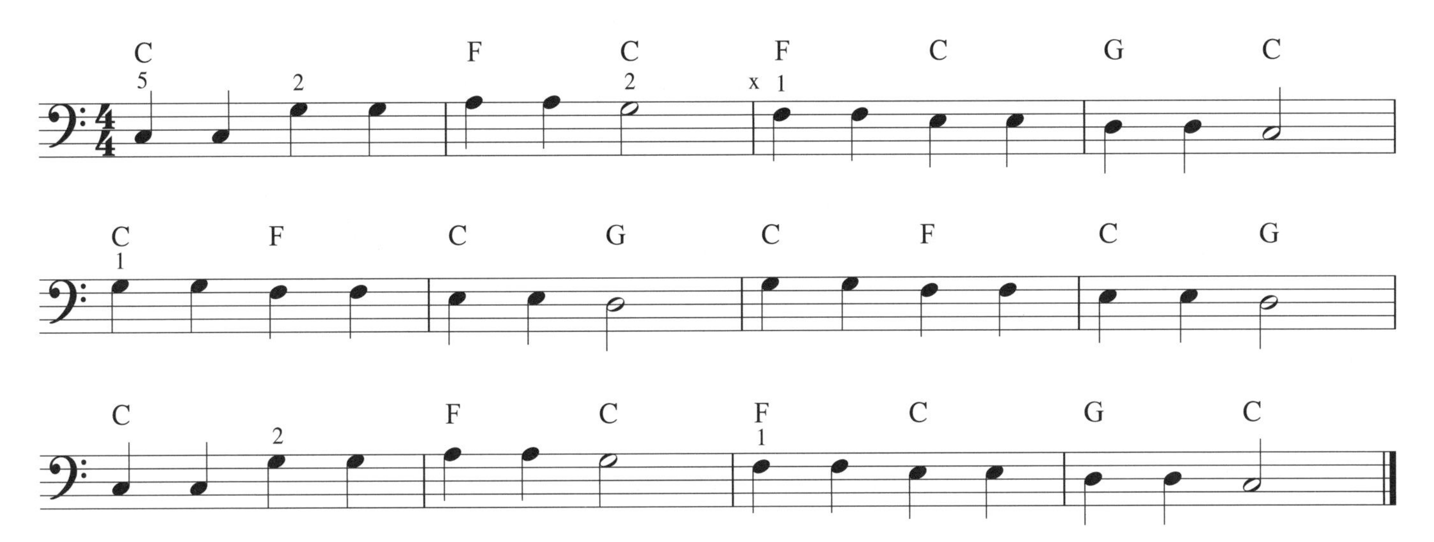

Using this lead sheet, try accompanying "Twinkle, Twinkle Little Star."

Here are the first four bars arranged several different ways. Continue the pattern all the way through the song by reading and playing the chords indicated above the melody in the same style used in each example.

Once you are proficient in playing an accompaniment this way, try singing the melody at the same time, or playing it one octave higher with your right hand. You may even find a friend to play the melody while you accompany them!

REVIEW

Play and say the names of these notes:

Name the notes below.

Name the intervals below using numbers 1–8. Then play these intervals.

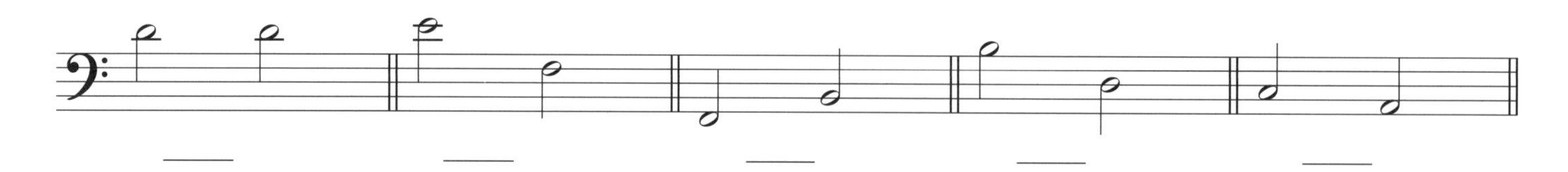

Name the inversions below. Use R for root position, "1" for first inversion (if the third is on the bottom), and "2" for second inversion (if the fifth of the chord is on the bottom.) Then play these chords.

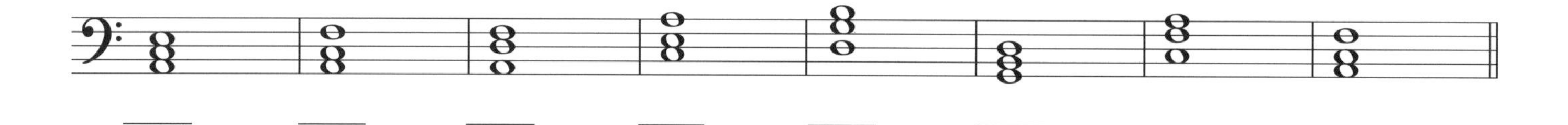

CHALLENGE

Name and rewrite the given chords in root position. To find the root, rearrange the notes until you are able to stack them in thirds (all lines or all spaces). The note that ends up on the bottom will be the root.

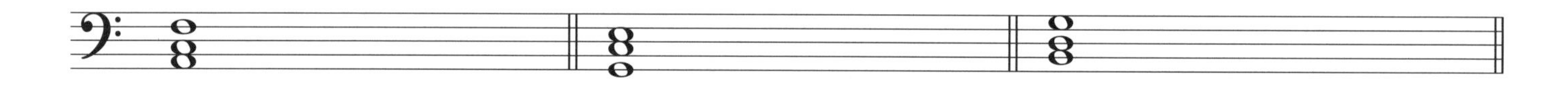

Enjoy playing a few more songs using the notes you have learned so far.

Happy Birthday

Overture from *The Nutcracker*

Pyotr Ilyich Tchaikovsky

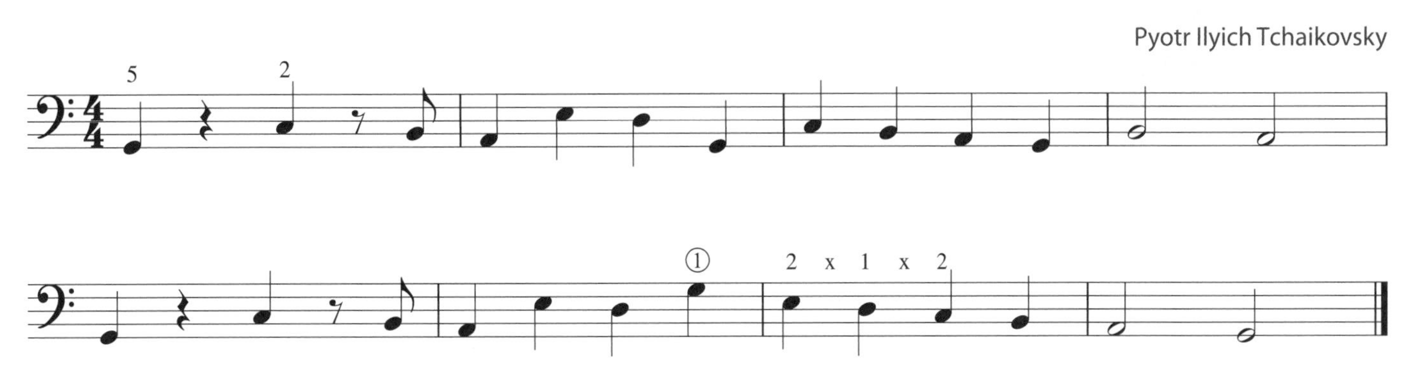

Fantasie-Impromptu, Second Movement Theme

Frédéric Chopin

CHALLENGE: Syncopation and Sixteenth Notes

Count several bars of quarter notes in 3/4 ("one, two, three") then count several bars of eighth notes in 3/4 ("one and two and three and"). Most of the notes in the first bar of the following piece fall on the "and" of the beat, rather than on the beat.

Also, notice the sixteenth notes at the beginning of the example. To count sixteenth notes, say "one e and a, two e and a, three e and a." The first notes of this piece fall on "three e and a." When preparing to start this piece, count two beats of sixteenth notes, "one e and a, two e and a," and then play from the beginning.

Play this melody from a string quartet by Boccherini.

Luigi Boccherini

LEARNING LOW C POSITION

- Learning Note Names from Low C to Low E
- Songs Using New Notes
- Bass Lines
- Seventh Chords
- Accompaniment Patterns
- Review

LEARNING NOTES FROM LOW C TO LOW E

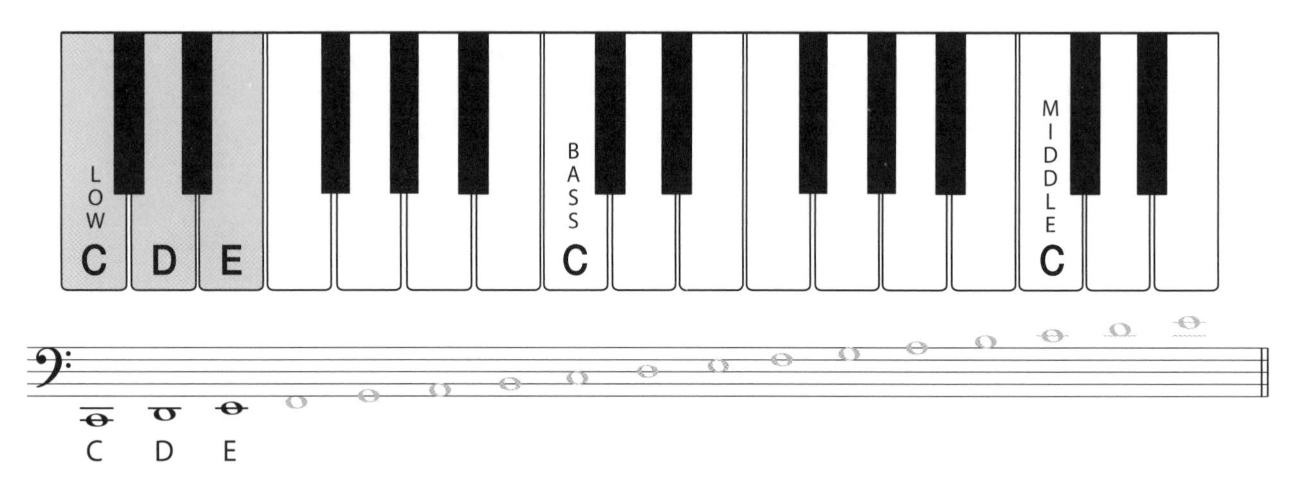

Chapter 3 covered notes down to the F just below the bass staff; now you're going to learn the three notes just below that. Remember that although ledger lines are used, they still count as line and space notes.

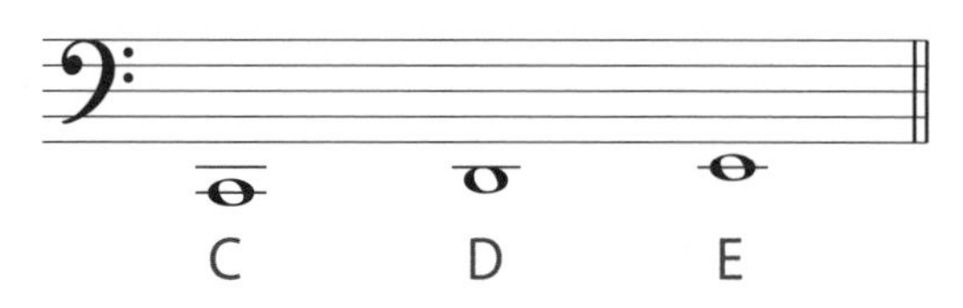

Draw these new notes below the staff using ledger lines.

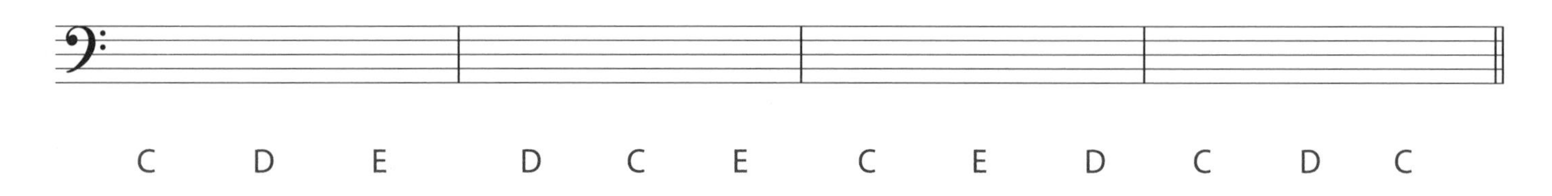

Practice these notes for fluency, starting with D and E. As always, say the note name as you play the exercise.

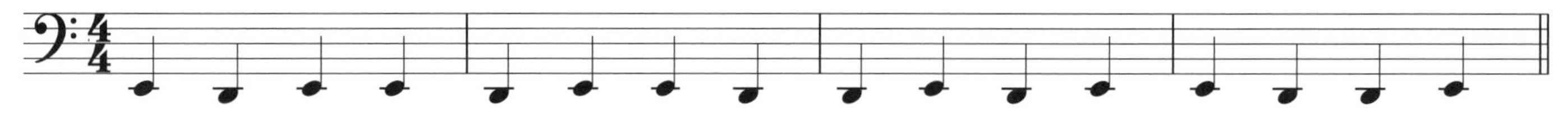

Now play C and D.

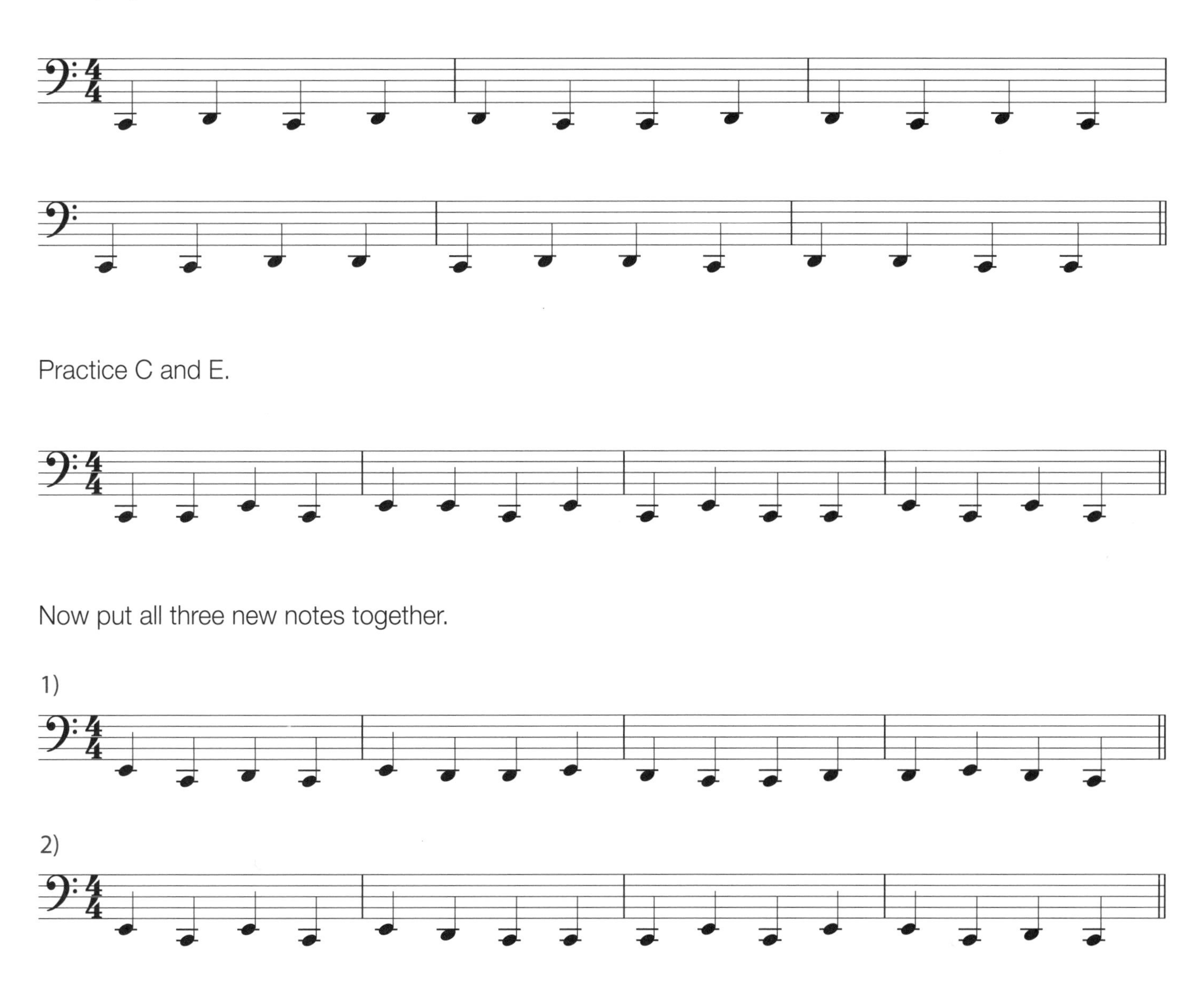

Practice C and E.

Now put all three new notes together.

1)

2)

Name the melodic interval indicated, then say and play each note. Remember, melodic means one note at a time, as in a melody. Use numbers 1–8.

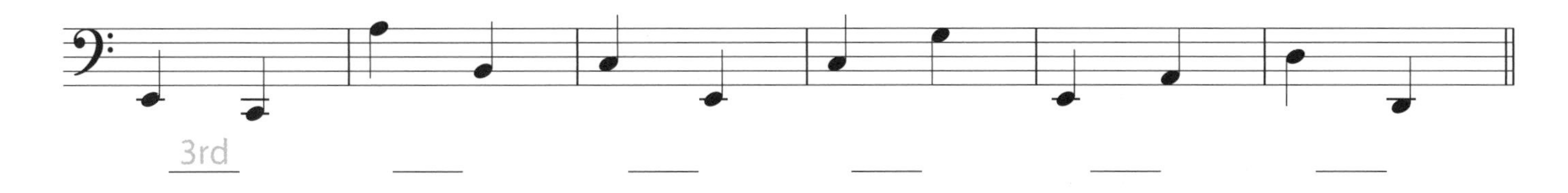

Draw a note above the given note to create the harmonic interval indicated, then write the name of the note you drew. Harmonic means more than one note at a time, so stack your note on top of the given note, touching the stem.

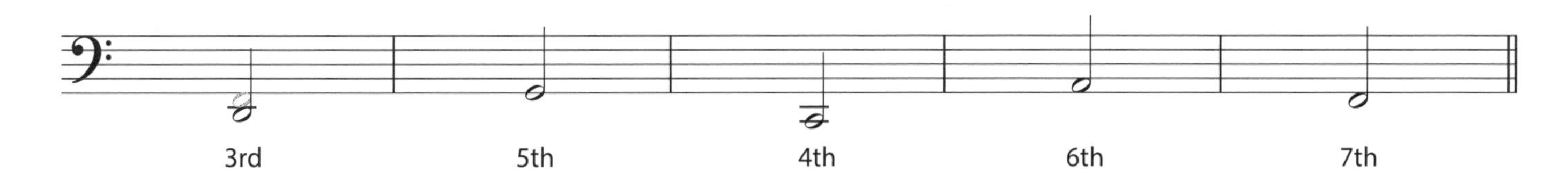

SONGS USING NEW NOTES

These songs include your new notes as well as notes from previous chapters.

SEVENTH CHORDS

So far, you have learned about chords which contain three notes: a root, a third and a fifth. These types of chords are referred to as as *triads*, because they have only three notes. Some chords contain four notes; in addition to their root, third and fifth, they also contain a *seventh*. Find this note by stacking an additional third on top of the triad.

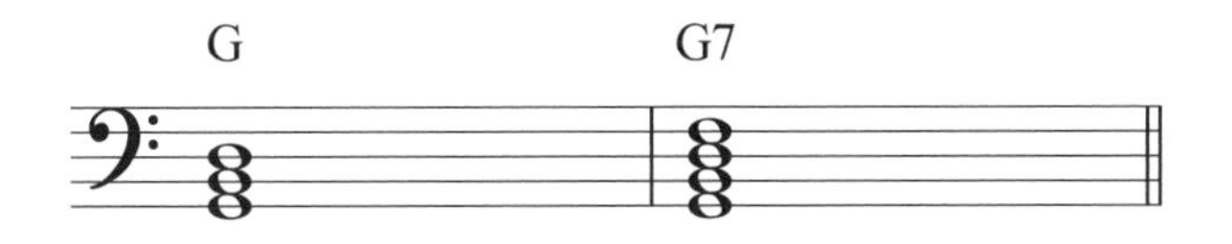

Just as there are different types of triads including major and minor, there are different types of seventh chords. The most important type is a major triad with minor third on top (a minor seventh away from the root). This is called a "dominant seventh" chord, and it is usually built on the fifth note of a major scale. Following is a C major scale, and a G dominant seventh chord:

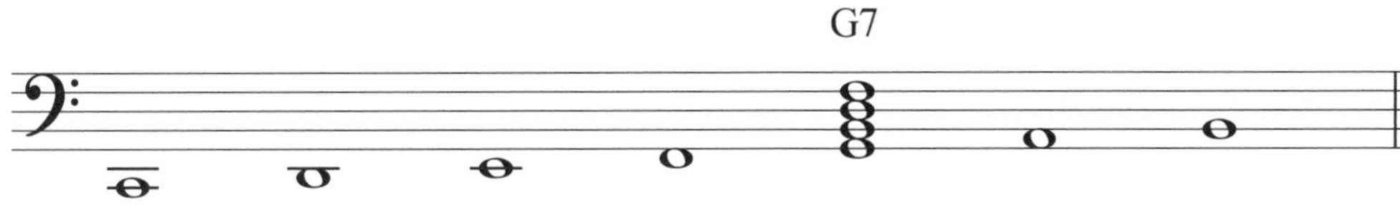

Notice it contains an F♮ instead of an F♯. This chord uses notes in C major, rather than the notes in G major.

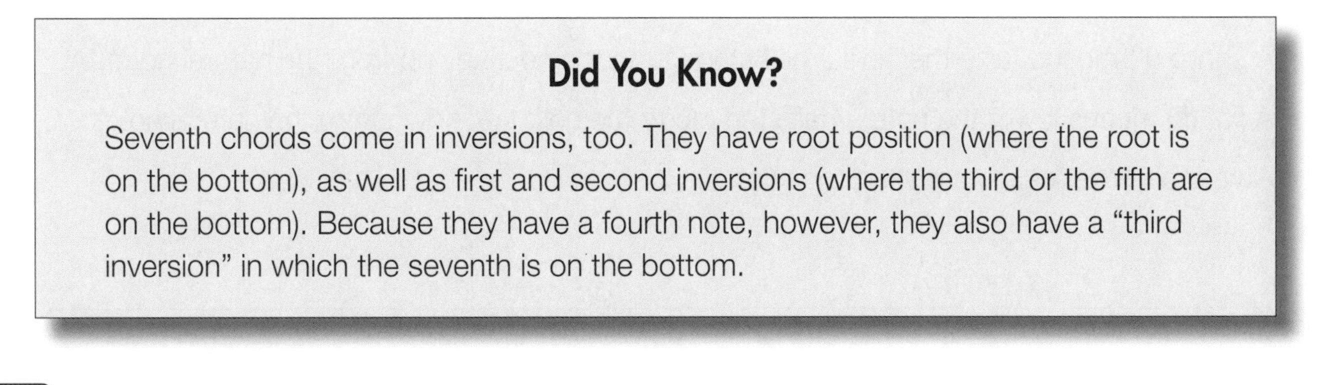

Did You Know?

Seventh chords come in inversions, too. They have root position (where the root is on the bottom), as well as first and second inversions (where the third or the fifth are on the bottom). Because they have a fourth note, however, they also have a "third inversion" in which the seventh is on the bottom.

CHALLENGE: Seventh Chord Inversions

Here is a seventh chord in root position. Notice that C is the root of the chord, E is the third, G is the fifth and B♭ is the seventh.

Here are different inversions of the same chord. If the third of the chord is on the bottom, it's a first inversion chord. If the fifth is on the bottom, it's a second inversion and if the seventh is on the bottom, it's a third inversion chord. In which inversions are these chords?
(Hint: The bottom note will tell you the inversion, no matter which octave it's in.)

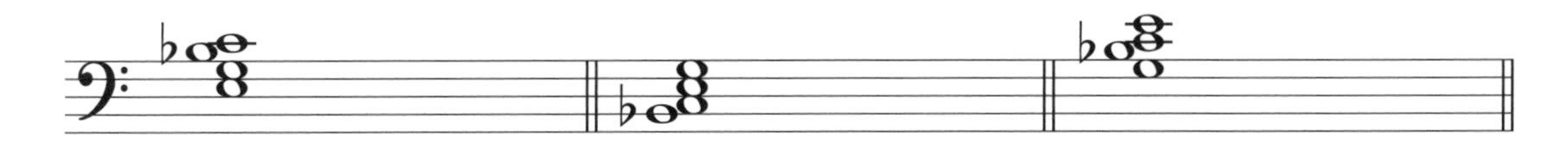

BASS LINES

A *bass line* is a melodic pattern played by an instrument with a low range, including the lower register of the piano. It is often repeated, but with notes changing to fit the chords of the piece or song.

A bass line has two important functions: One function is to show the harmony. A simple way to accomplish this in a bass line is to simply play the notes of the chord; this is called "outlining" a chord. Name these intervals, then say and play these notes.

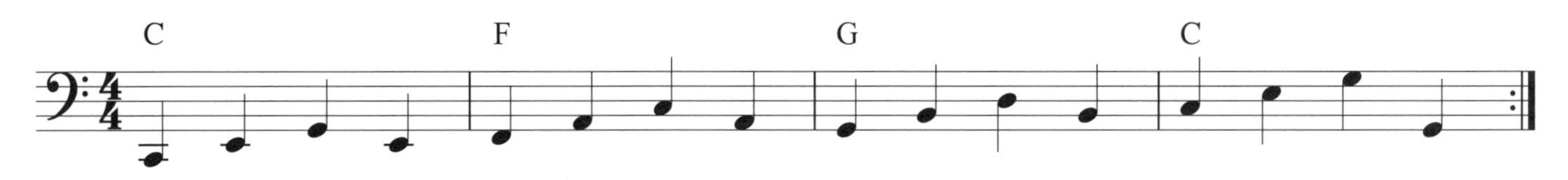

The other important job of a bass line is to show the beat and style, or feel, of the type of music you're playing. The bass line above is called a "walking" bass line, because it has a steady rhythm. This is common in jazz, as well as many other types of non-classical music.

Below is a twelve-bar blues bass line. Sometimes the chords are outlined, and other times scale tones are used. As long as chord tones are played on the important beats 1 and 3, and the other notes are within the key, the harmony will still make sense. Scales make the bass line feel even more like "walking," as they provide a sense of forward momentum.

Say and play the notes. Remember:

- A sharp (♯) means raise the note a half step (go to the next key up from the natural note).
- A flat (♭) means lower the note a half step (go to the next key down from the natural note).
- A natural (♮) cancels out a sharp or a flat.

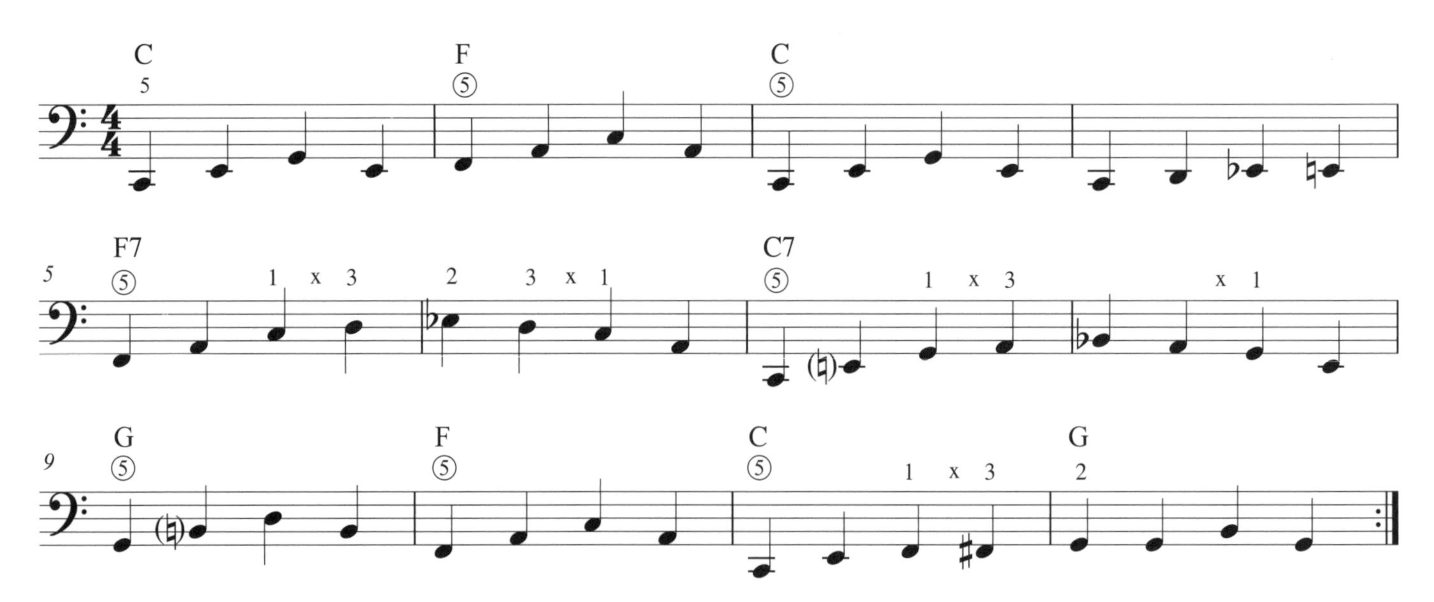

Chromatic Passing Tones

In jazz, half steps are used extensively to lead from one chord to another. We call these "chromatic passing tones," because they use a chromatic scale to pass from one chord to another. You can see evidence of this in bars 4 and 11 above, as the notes near the end of those bars lead up in half steps to land on the roots of the chords in the following bars.

Swing Rhythm

Sometimes eighth notes need to be played with a "swing" feel. This means to play a triplet rhythm instead of an even rhythm. The opposite of playing "swing" is playing "straight."

A rhythm played straight is played exactly as written, with all eighth notes played evenly. Each note lasts the same amount of time as the others.

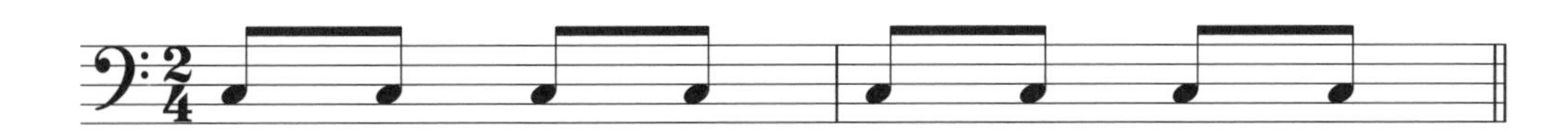

A swing rhythm is played unevenly, with a "long-short, long-short" rhythm. The rhythm will be written exactly the same way as the previous example, but will be played like this:

Swing this!

ACCOMPANIMENT PATTERNS

Play these accompaniment patterns in both styles: first straight, then swing.

CHALLENGE: Tension and Resolution

In music, we call the chord of the home key the "tonic" chord. For example, if a piece of music is in C major, the tonic is the note C and the tonic chord is C major.

Dominant seventh chords really make us want to hear the tonic afterwards; because of this, in classical music, the dominant seventh chord has to be followed by a chord with the tonic note in it (usually the tonic chord.) Try playing this G dominant seventh chord followed by a C major chord. You'll hear the tension in the G7 chord being "resolved" to the C major chord.

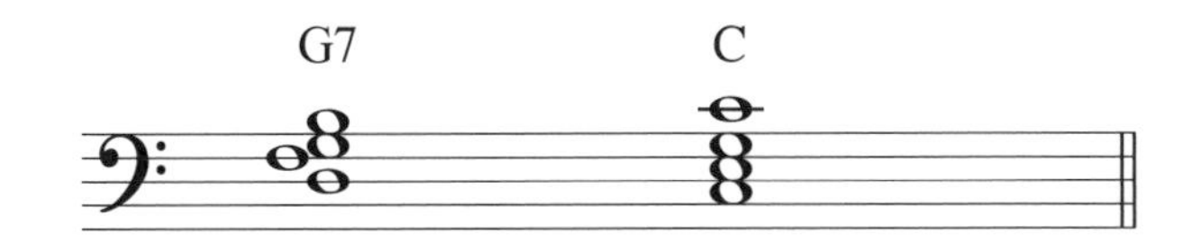

REVIEW

Say and play these notes. Work out your own fingering using the skills you've developed in previous exercises.

Name the notes below, then play the exercise.

Name the intervals below. Then, say and play these notes.

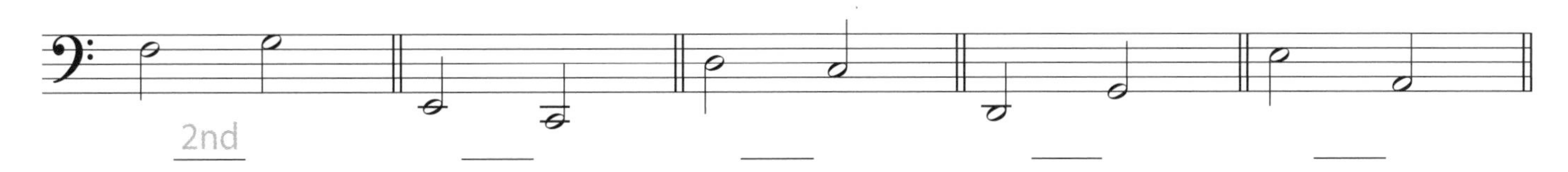

Name the inversions below. Use R for root position, 1 for first inversion (if the third is on the bottom), and 2 for second inversion (if the fifth of the chord is on the bottom.) Then, play these chords.

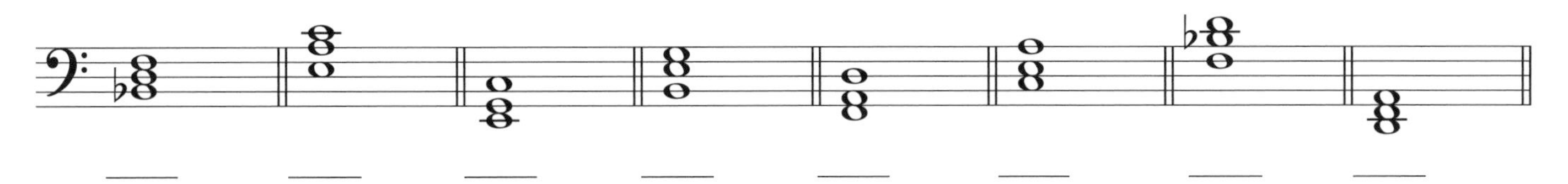

CHALLENGE: Analyze This!

Play these chord progressions and name the inversions.

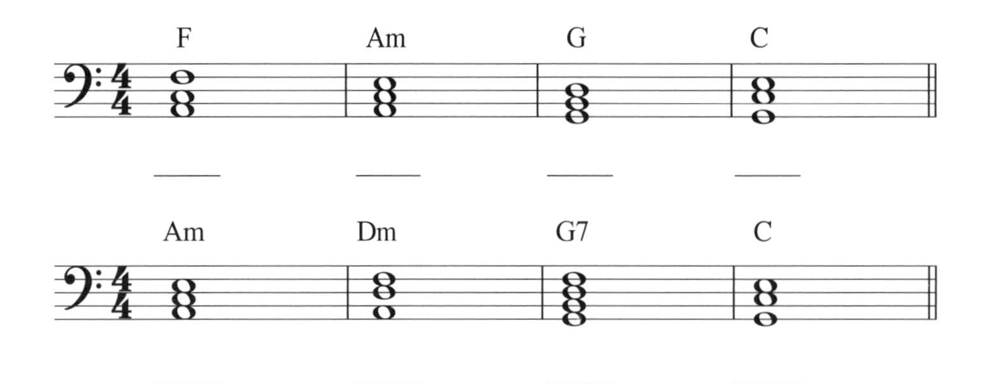

Practice the notes you've learned so far.

If You're Happy and You Know It Clap Your Hands

READING LOW G POSITION

- Learning Note Names from G to B Below the Staff
- Songs Using New Notes
- Accompaniment Patterns
- Review

LEARNING NOTE NAMES FROM G TO B BELOW THE STAFF

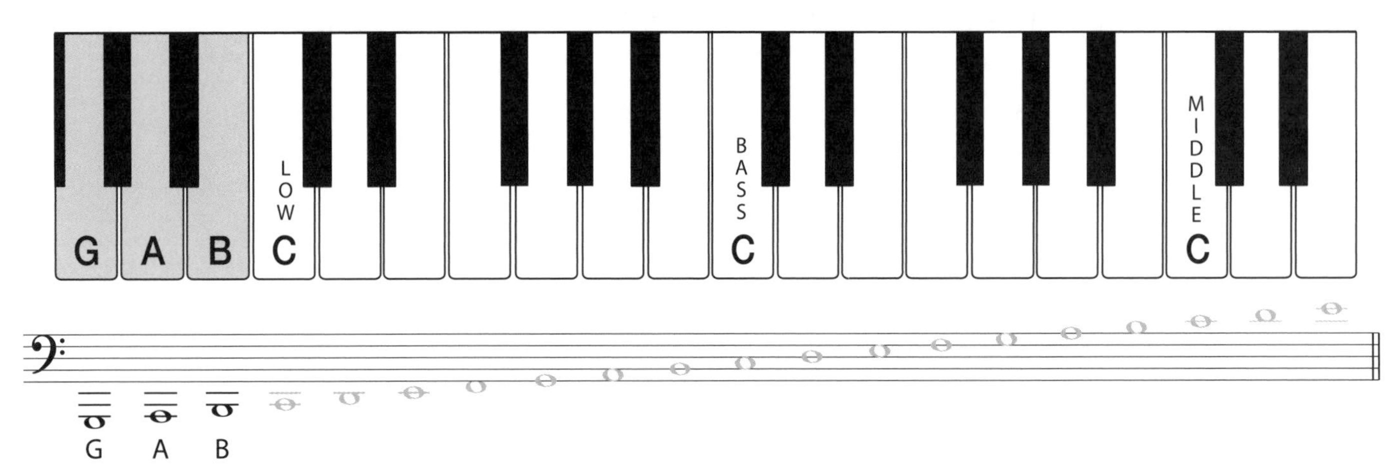

The final three notes covered in this book all appear on ledger lines.

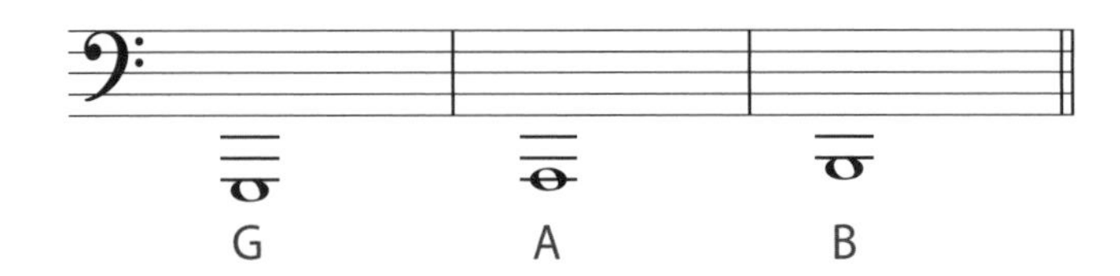

Draw these new notes below the staff using ledger lines.

Practice these notes for fluency, starting with A and B. As always, *say* the note name as you play.

Now play G and A.

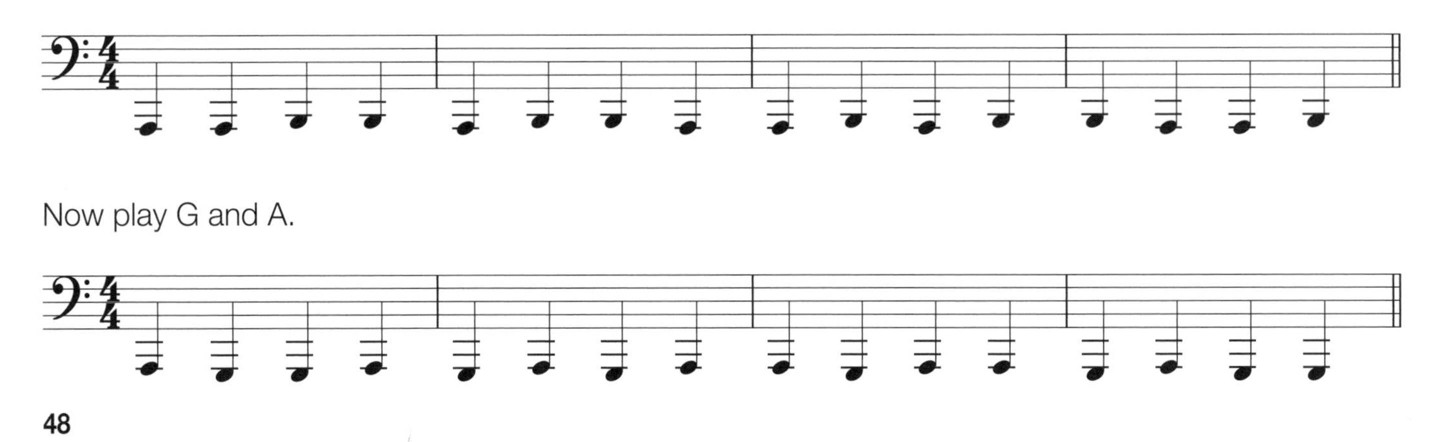

Now only G and B.

Put all three notes together.

Name the melodic interval indicated, then say and play each note.

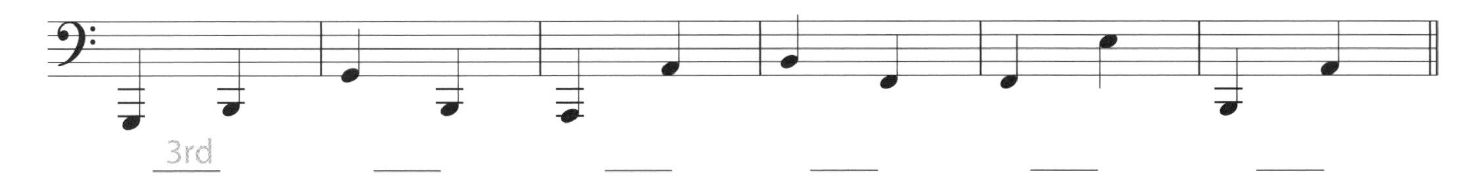

Draw a note above the given note to create the harmonic interval indicated below, then write the name of the note you drew.

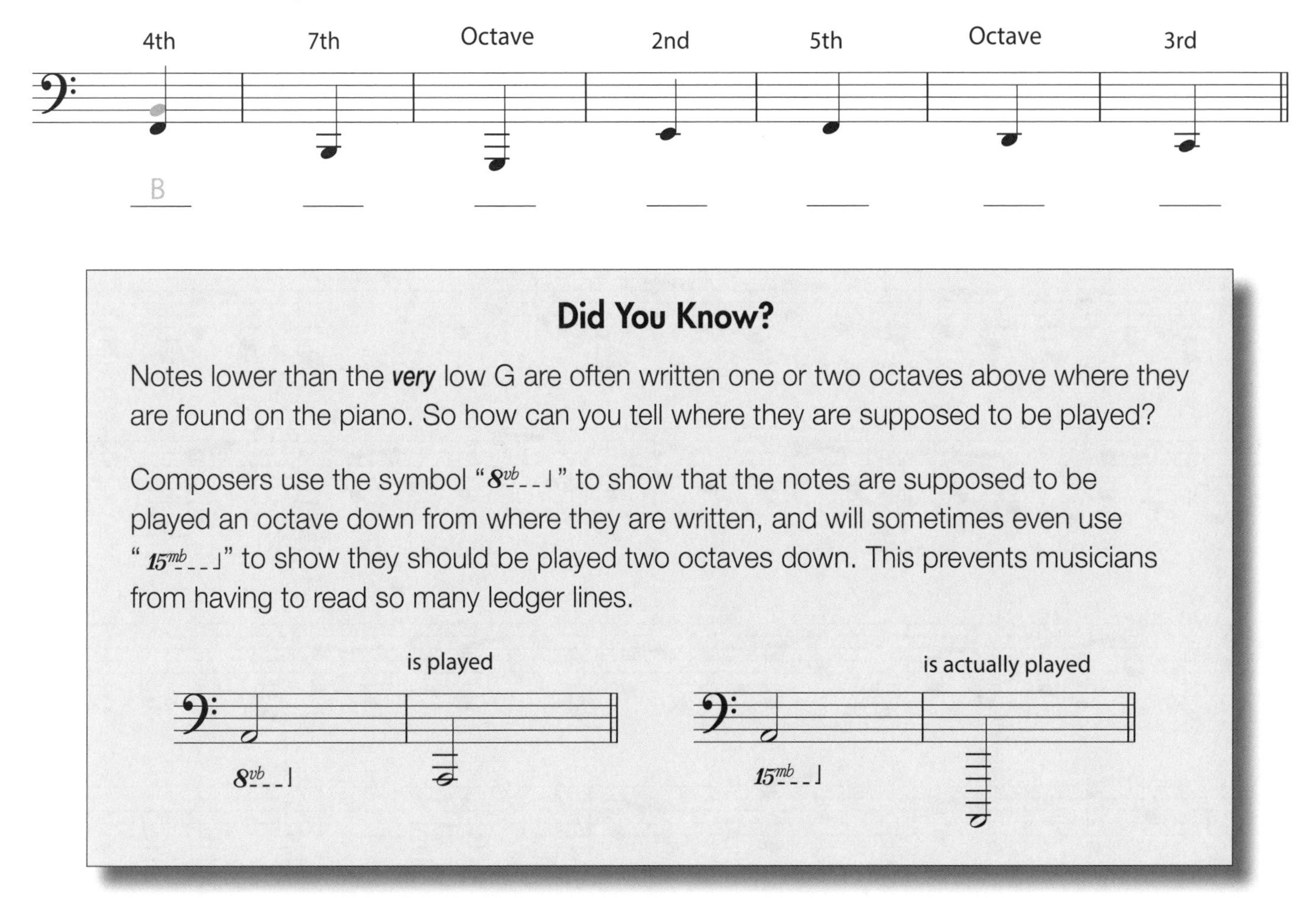

Did You Know?

Notes lower than the ***very*** low G are often written one or two octaves above where they are found on the piano. So how can you tell where they are supposed to be played?

Composers use the symbol "*8vb*- - ⌋" to show that the notes are supposed to be played an octave down from where they are written, and will sometimes even use "*15mb*- - ⌋" to show they should be played two octaves down. This prevents musicians from having to read so many ledger lines.

SONGS USING NEW NOTES

These songs add new notes to those learned in previous chapters.

For He's a Jolly Good Fellow

Theme from *Surprise Symphony* (Second Movement)

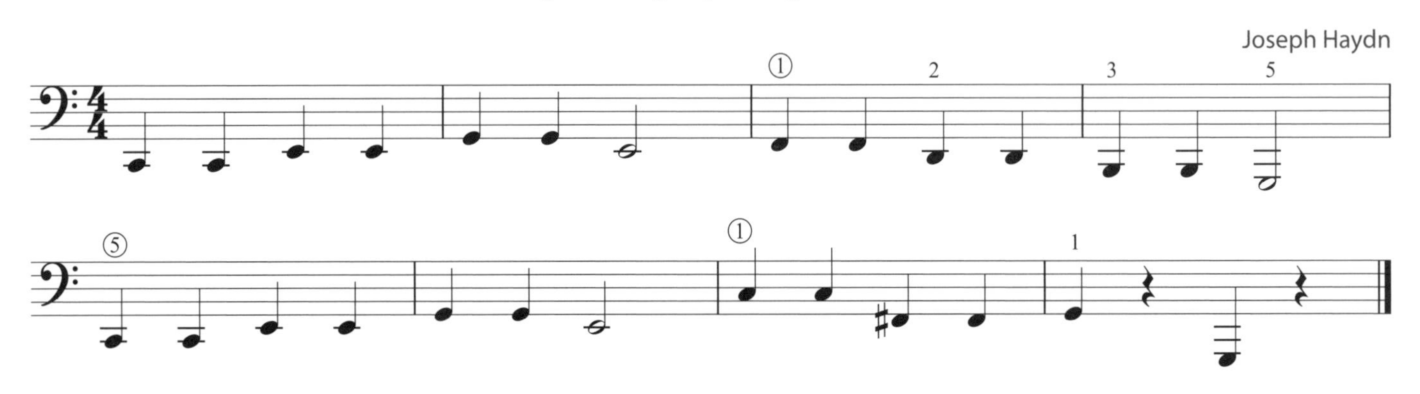

ACCOMPANIMENT PATTERNS

Typically, notes lower than Low C are not used in playing melodies in the left hand; they are simply too low to hear clearly. However, this lowest register of the piano is perfect for bass lines.

When used together with notes an octave up, the lowest notes on the piano add volume and power, and the higher-octave notes make it easier to hear the melody or other pattern you're playing. This effect works whether notes are played together or separately. It's a winning combination!

CHALLENGE: Stride Piano

Stride is a style of piano playing that was developed in Harlem in the 1920s, with roots in ragtime. It involves playing the melody in the right hand, and alternating between a bass note and chord in the left hand. Play these two stride piano accompaniment patterns using only your left hand.

REVIEW

Say and play these notes.

Name the harmonic intervals below, then say and play the notes.

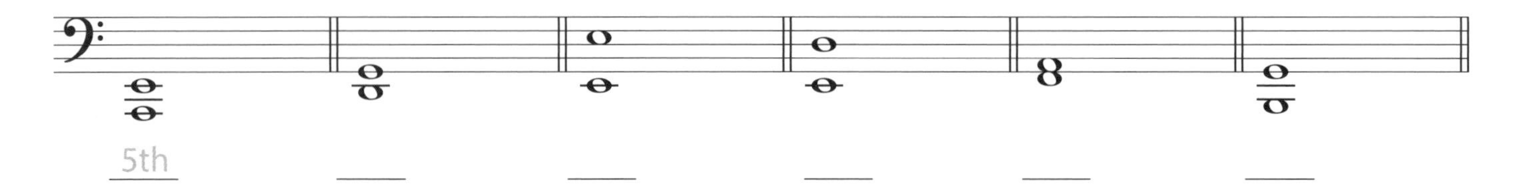

Name the melodic intervals below, then say and play the notes.

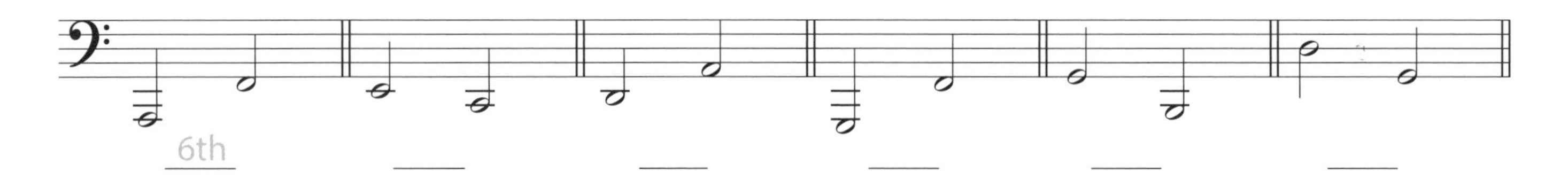

Name the inversions below. Use R for root position, 1 for first inversion (if the third is on the bottom), and 2 for second inversion (if the fifth of the chord is on the bottom.)

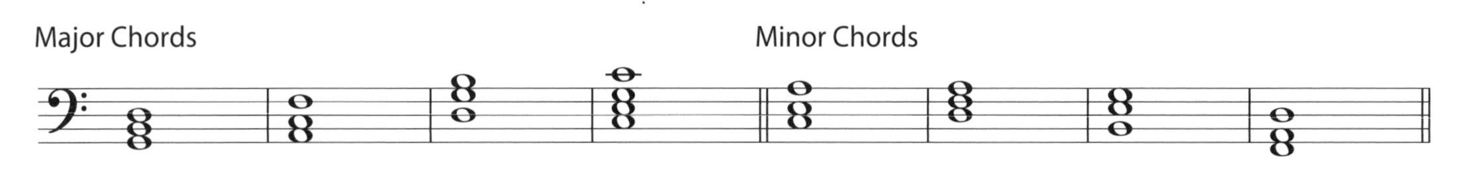

CHALLENGE

Name the chords above. Your options are C, F, or G for major chords, and Dm, Em, or Am for minor chords.

(Hint: Change the octaves of the notes in a chord until the chord is in root position. Then, the note on the bottom will be the root.)

You have now learned nearly three octaves of notes in the bass clef. Congratulations! Enjoy playing more songs and accompaniment patterns that use your new knowledge.

My Bonnie Lies Over the Ocean

CHALLENGE: Key Signatures and Accidentals

A *key signature* is the set of symbols that appears after the clef at the beginning of each line of music. The key signature defines the key you're playing in by illustrating which notes are to be played as sharps or flats. Notice the two sharps next to the bass clef in the song below. These two sharps are F♯ and C♯, and this key signature tells you that all the notes in this piece will be natural letters except for F and C (and those altered by accidentals). Use this challenge to try to play within the confines of a key signature in preparation for Chapter 6.

In the Hall of the Mountain King

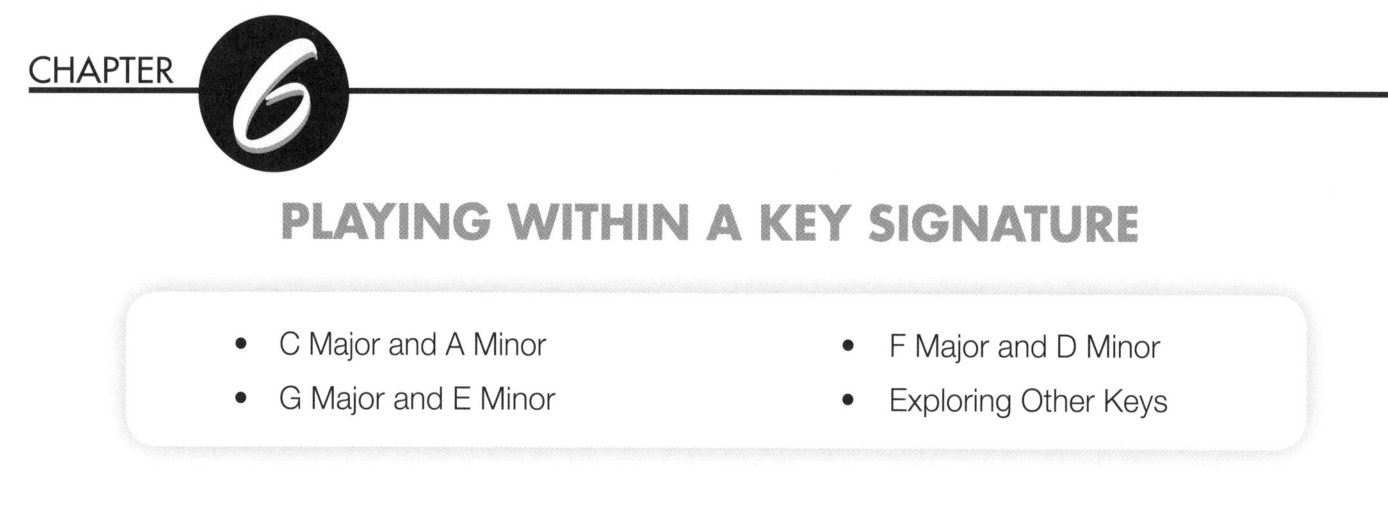

PLAYING WITHIN A KEY SIGNATURE

- C Major and A Minor
- G Major and E Minor
- F Major and D Minor
- Exploring Other Keys

C MAJOR AND A MINOR

C Major

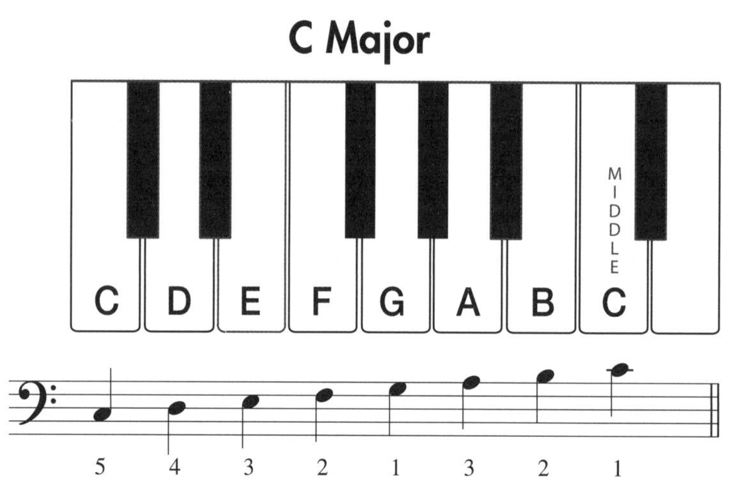

A key signature with no sharps or flats means that you will use only white keys unless you see an accidental. This is the key signature for C major and its relative minor, A minor.

Accompaniment Chords and Patterns

When Irish Eyes Are Smiling (Melody)

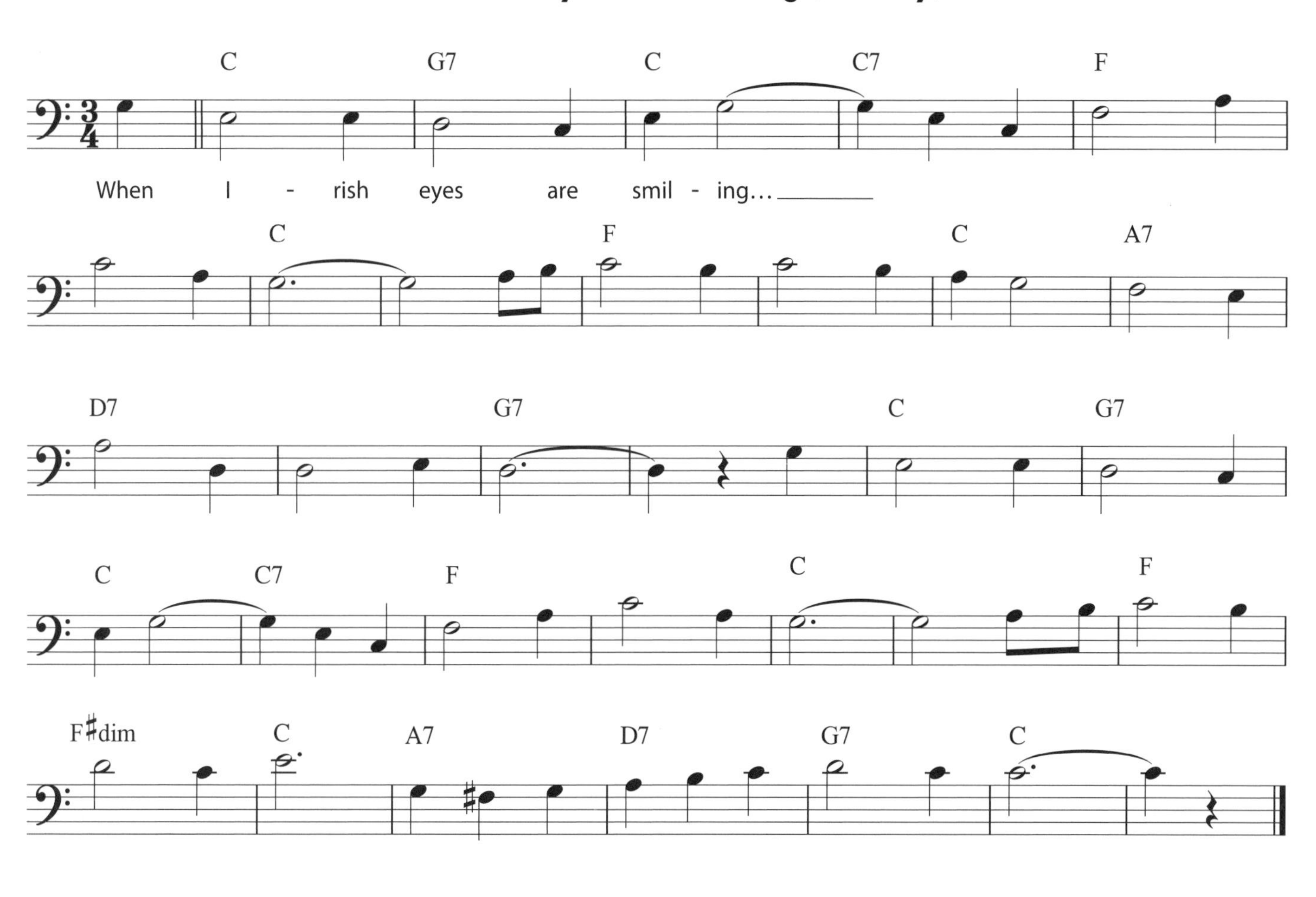

When Irish Chords Are Broken (Accompaniment)

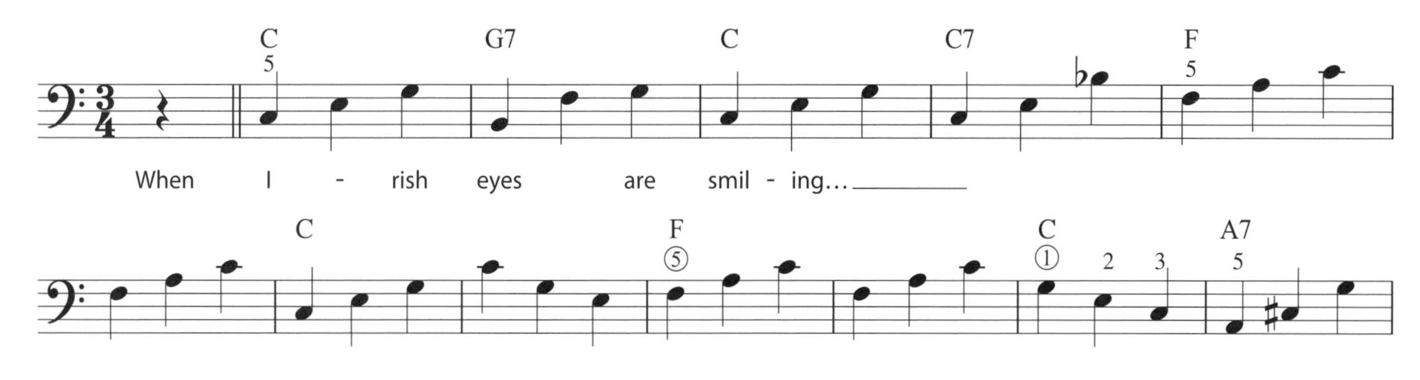

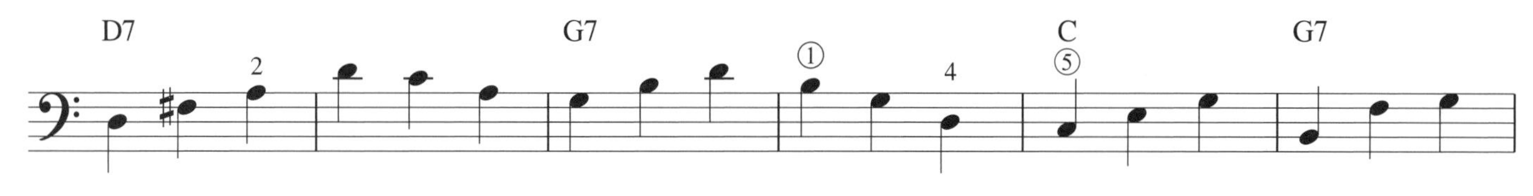

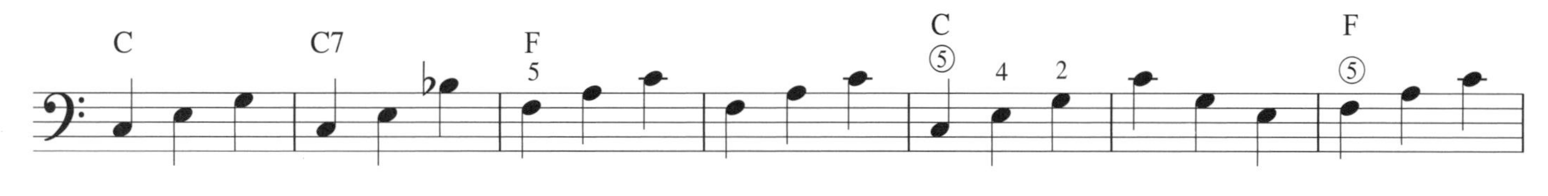

A Minor

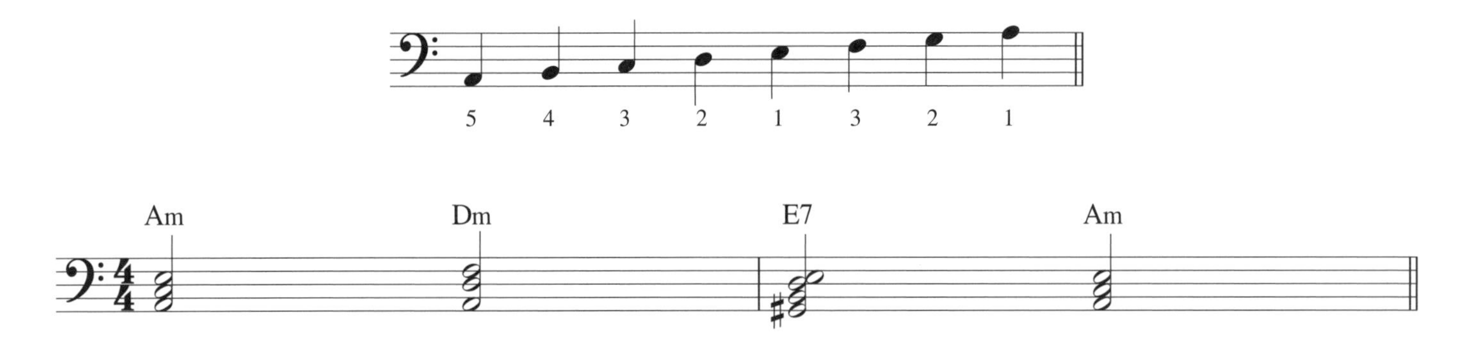

The dominant seventh chord is so important in music that minor keys often "borrow" a note from their major keys. The key of A minor borrows a G♯ from A major to make an E7 chord, as shown in the progression above. If this is not done, the chord that exists naturally in A minor is E minor, as shown in the song below.

Sakura (Melody)

Sakura (Accompaniment)

G MAJOR AND E MINOR

G Major

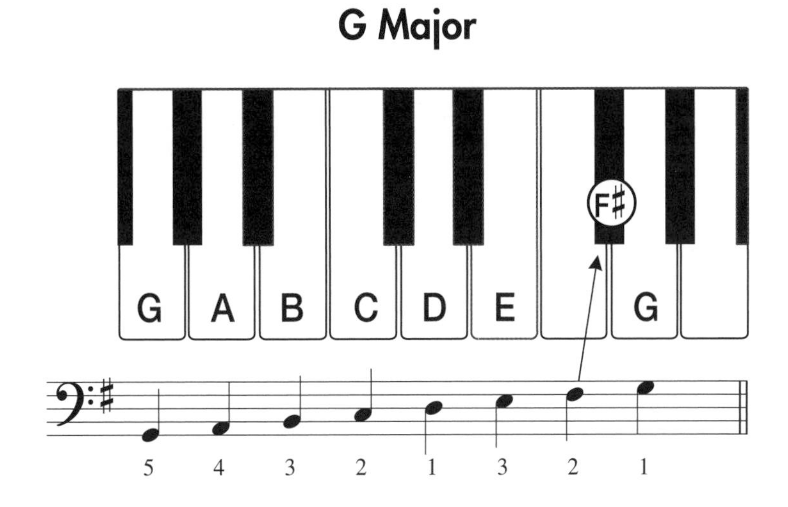

A key signature with one sharp and no flats means that only white keys are used, except for F which is played F♯. This is the key signature for G major and its relative minor, E minor.

Accompaniment Chords and Patterns

Take Me out to the Ball Game (Melody)

Notice the new chord symbols used in this piece. The symbols "maj7" and "m7" (short for "major seventh" and "minor seventh") show that the qualities of these seventh chords are different than the dominant seventh chord you learned about in Chapter 4. Although they are built the same way by stacking notes in thirds on top of the root, these types of chords do not make the listener need to hear the tonic afterwards.

The symbol "6" means that the sixth scale degree is used to form the chord instead of the seventh. This means that the chord was formed by stacking a second on top of a triad rather than another third.

F MAJOR AND D MINOR

F Major

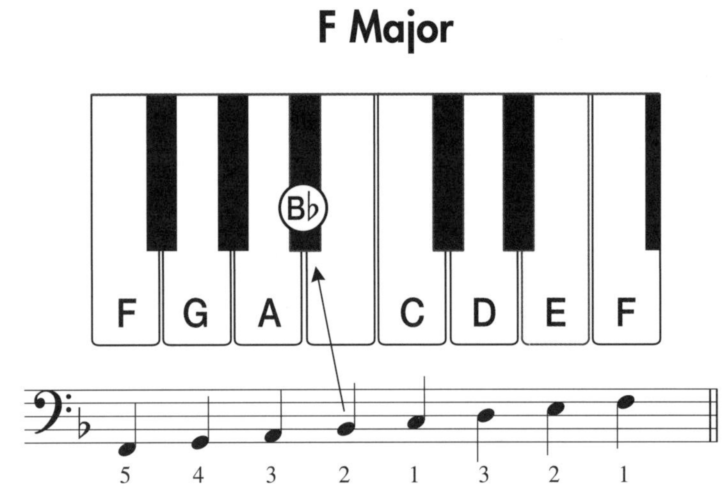

A key signature with one flat and no sharps indicates all white notes are played except for B, which is played B♭. This is the key signature for F major and its relative minor, D minor.

Accompaniment Chords and Patterns

This Old Man (Accompaniment)

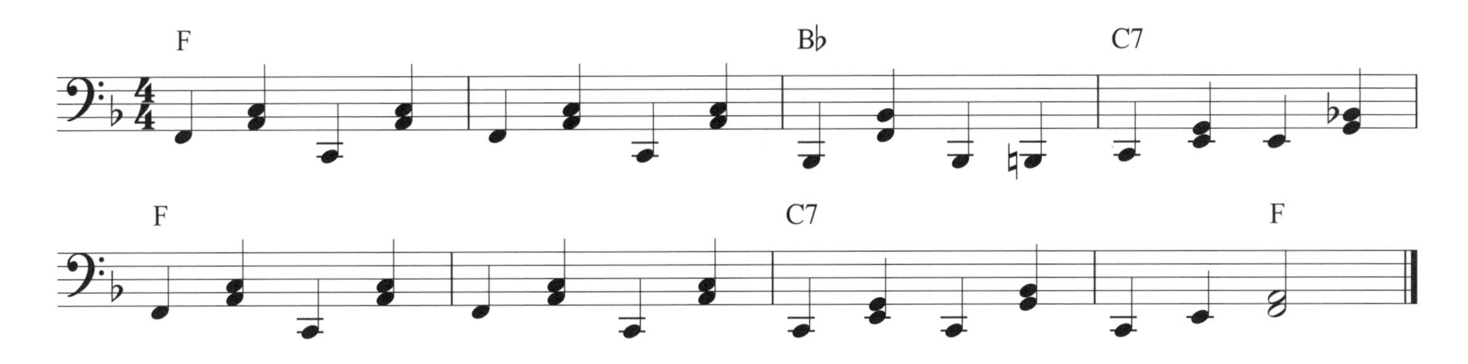

Amazing Grace (Melody)

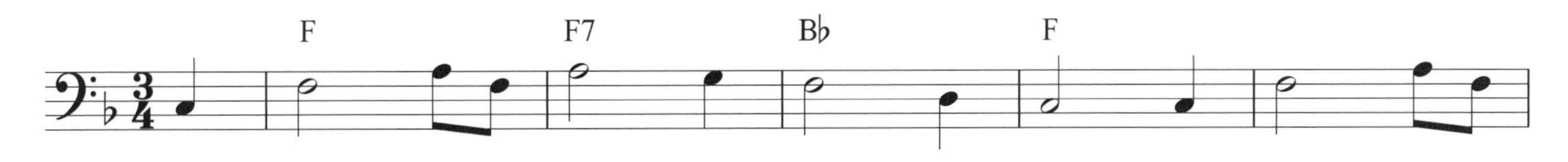

Amazing Grace (Accompaniment)

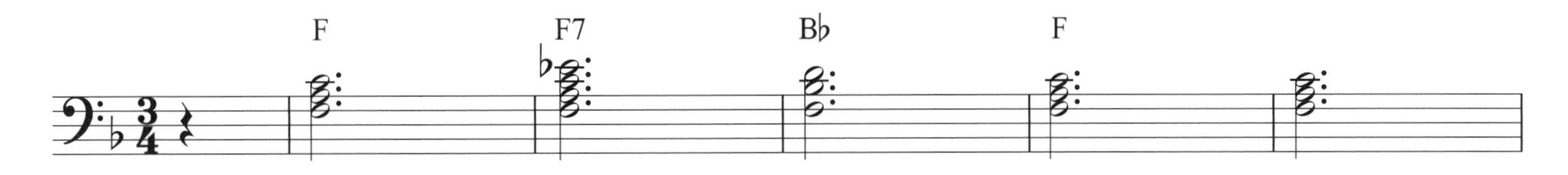

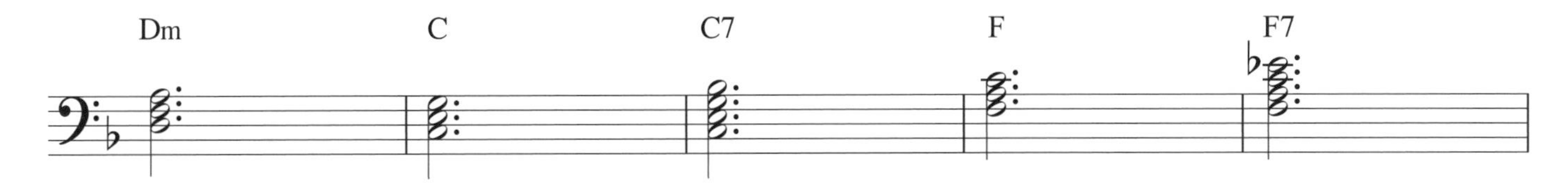

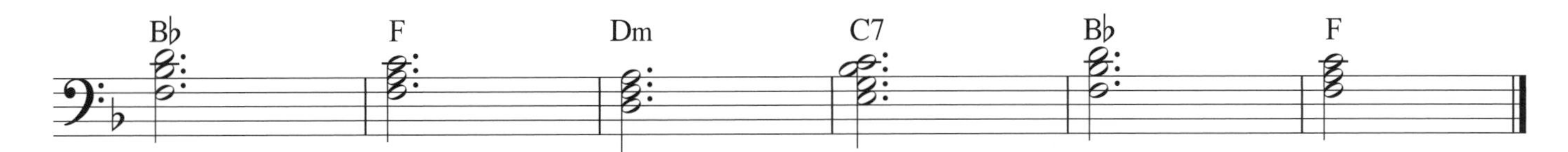

D Minor

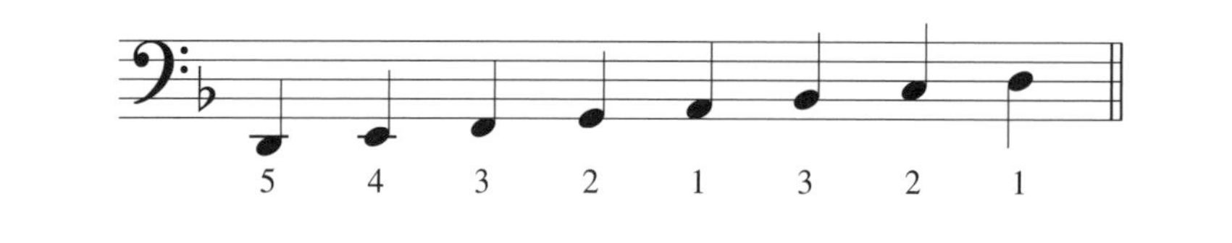

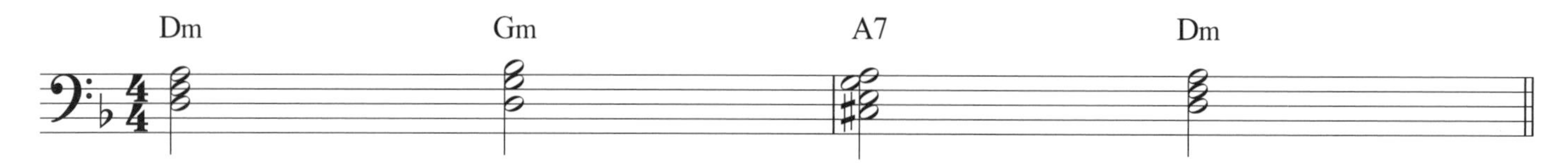

Wayfaring Stranger (Melody)

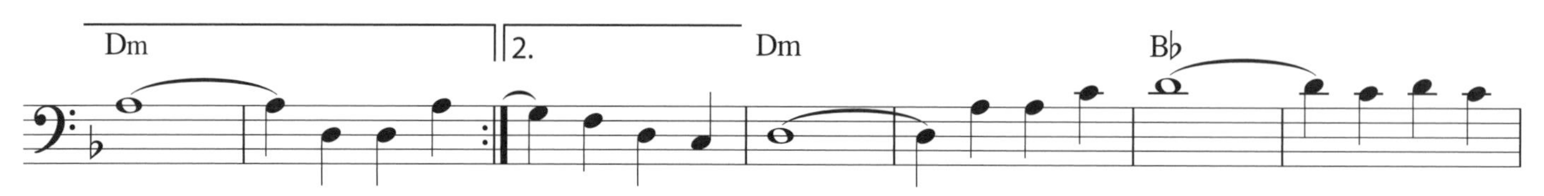

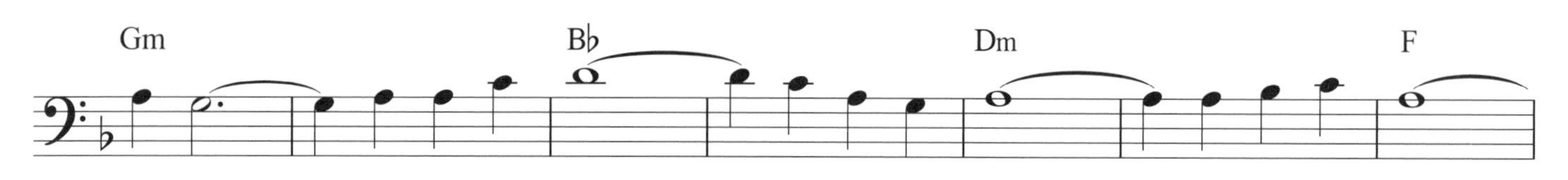

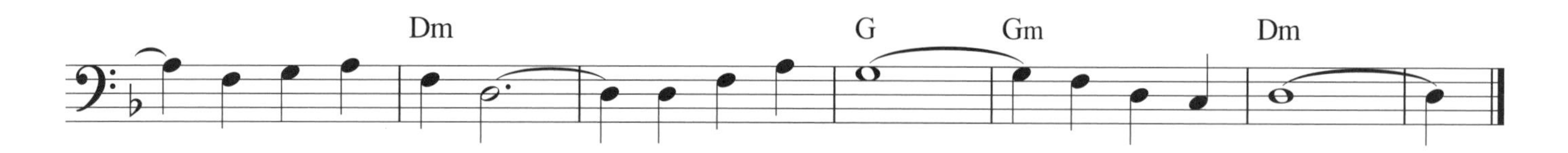

Wayfaring Stranger (Accompaniment)

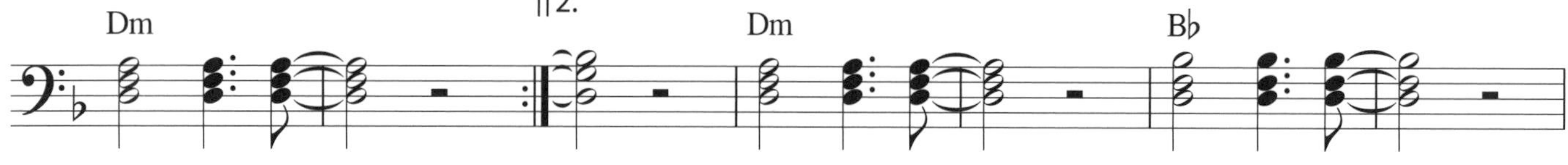

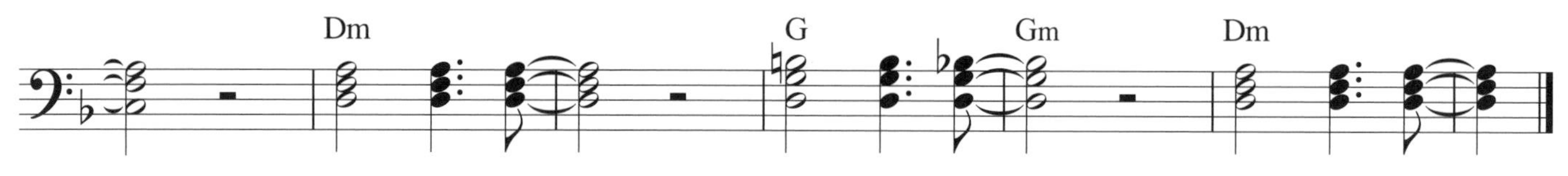

EXPLORING OTHER KEYS

In Chapter 6 you become well-acquainted with three keys. Now it's time to test your knowledge of the bass clef by reading accidentals through all twelve major keys. Play and say the notes in this bass line.

Play the same progression in block chords.

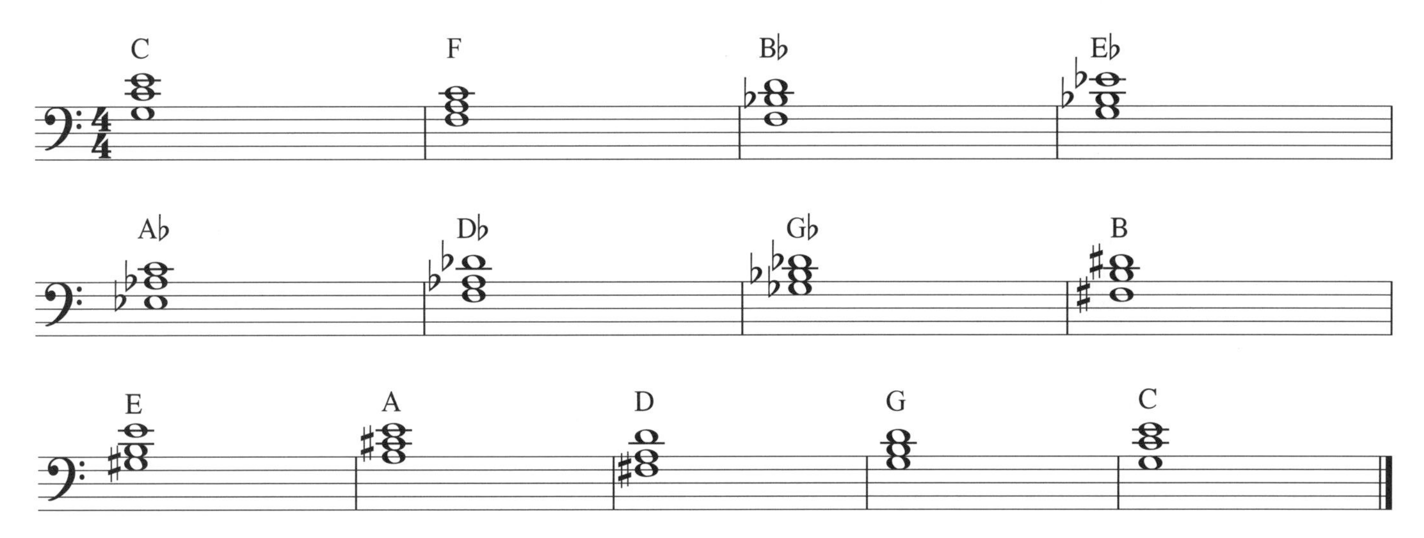

Congratulations! By now you have the tools for a solid understanding not only of how to read and play notes in the bass clef, but also of how the left hand functions in piano playing. These new skills will serve you well for years to come. We wish you all the best on your piano journey!

ABOUT THE AUTHORS

Photo by Jordan Hayes

Caroline McCaskey, a native daughter of the genre-bending West Coast music scene, is equally at home in the traditional, improvising and classical music worlds. With each engaging performance, Caroline draws from her degrees in music composition and performance, as well as from her long history performing with Alasdair Fraser and the San Francisco Scottish Fiddlers (which she joined at age 12). She also performs throughout the U.S. with the Contra, Scottish and English dance band StringFire!

In high demand as a teacher of both traditional and classical music, Caroline can be found teaching and performing at camps throughout the U.S. and Canada. She has taught piano, fiddle, violin, viola, cello, musical saw and theremin. She is certified by the Suzuki Association of the Americas to teach Violin books 1–10, and maintains an engaged and enthusiastic private lesson studio. Also a curriculum author, Caroline released the second edition of her well-regarded *AltStrings Fiddle Method for Violin, Viola, Cello* and *Bass Books 1* and *2* in early 2020.

Caroline would like to thank Nicola Marchi, Patti Cobb and Deborah McCaskey for their help and encouragement.

Charylu Roberts, Owner, O.Ruby Productions, has combined her musical knowledge, performance and teaching experience with design, illustration, editing and music typesetting skills to create, design and produce music books for the publishing industry since 1990. She has contributed to over 700 books and instructional videos.

Her clients have included the "Who's Who" of music print companies, music magazines, textbook publishers, and instructional music video companies, including: Hal Leonard, Alfred Music Publications, Mel Bay Publications, Homespun Music Instruction, Korg, Berklee Press, and Musicians Institute. She enjoys helping authors and educators design and develop projects, assisting them in getting their books out into the world.

As a lifelong keyboard player in a multitude of styles, Charylu has performed throughout the world and teaches piano privately in the San Francisco Bay Area.

Charylu would like to thank Jeff Schroedl and all the folks at Hal Leonard.